TRANSFORMED INTO A DRAGON!

Through your own careless experimentation with powerful magic, you, Treon, have somehow managed to transform yourself into the awesome form of a gigantic golden dragon!

Your strange new form may well provide you with the powers you will need to defeat the evil Crimson Wizard, whose weird hordes of lava warriors even now menace the gates of your home city. But if you remain in your present form for too long, the spell that transformed you into a dragon may become permanent!

What will you do?

1) If you decide to try to regain your human form now, so as not to risk spending the rest of your life as a dragon, turn to page 145.

2) If you decide to remain a dragon long enough to fight the Crimson Wizard and take a chance on not being able to become human again, turn to page 101.

Whichever choice you make, you are sure to find adventure, as you are taken
UNDER DRAGON'S WING

Under
Dragon's Wing

BY JOHN KENDALL

A DUNGEONS & DRAGONS™ ADVENTURE BOOK

Cover Art by Elmore
Interior Art by Sam Grainger

TSR, Inc.
PRODUCTS OF YOUR IMAGINATION™

To Liz, because she's special

UNDER DRAGON'S WING
©Copyright 1984, TSR, Inc.
All Rights Reserved.

Distributed to the book trade in the United States by Random House, Inc., and in Canada by Random House of Canada, Ltd.

Distributed in the United Kingdom by TSR (UK), Ltd. Distributed to the toy and hobby trade by regional distributors.

DUNGEONS & DRAGONS, ENDLESS QUEST, and PICK A PATH TO ADVENTURE are trademarks owned by TSR, Inc.

D&D is a registered trademark owned by TSR, Inc.

First printing: February, 1984
Printed in the United States of America
Library of Congress Catalog Card Number: 83-91423
ISBN: 0-88038-076-4

9 8 7 6 5 4 3 2 1

TSR, Inc.
P.O. Box 756
Lake Geneva, WI 53147

TSR (UK), Ltd.
The Mill, Rathmore Road
Cambridge CB1 4AD
United Kingdom

ou are about to set off on an adventure in which YOU will meet many dangers—and face many decisions. YOUR choices will determine how the story turns out. So be careful . . . you must choose wisely!

Do not read this book from beginning to end! Instead, as you are faced with a decision, follow the instructions and keep turning to the pages where your choices lead you until you come to an end. At any point, YOUR choice could bring success—or disaster!

You can read UNDER DRAGON'S WING many times, with many different results, so if you make an unwise choice, go back to the beginning and start again!

Good luck on YOUR adventure!

In this story, you are Treon, young prince of the proud kingdom of Grendopolan. With your country besieged on all sides by the armies of the evil Crimson Wizard, your parents have sent you and your elf tutor Rynath to the far-off town of Trigedium for your own safety. But you cannot be satisfied until you discover a way to come to the aid of your country in its hour of great crisis. . . .

"But I am a prince of Grendopolan!" you complain, your voice rising. "An apprentice wizard, too. How could my parents possibly have sent me off to this backwoods village, hundreds of miles from home, just because I blundered one little spell!"

You angrily trudge down half-empty streets through the marketplace of Trigedium.

"Treon, we are supposed to keep your identity a secret," your elven tutor, Rynath, whispers sharply. "And coming here has nothing to do with your bungled web spell! Your parents thought you would be safer here than in Balshad while our country is under attack," she adds.

You glare back at her in disbelief as she continues.

"Your parents need all the soldiers they have, so they decided not to send any to guard you. You MUST agree to stay in disguise. With your road-muddied face and rough clothes, you're safe as long as you don't give yourself away. So keep your voice down!"

You look at the stern elf and feel your anger seep away. At the castle, Rynath is responsible for teaching you. You recall with fondness the many stolen moments for her patient chess lessons tucked among your other studies. But when you travel, the two-hundred-year-old elf also serves as your bodyguard. She can use her long sword, Glitteredge, with deadly accuracy, and keeps a cool head when danger threatens.

"I guess I should stick to reading about dragons and studying my lessons," you say, obediently lowering your voice. "Then maybe the next time there's trouble I can stay in Balshad to help out."

You move dejectedly on down the row of shops. Then your eye is caught by a small bookery. Stopping, you read the sign over the door:

MADAME URSULA—SPELLS, BOOKS, AND JEWELRY OF ANTIQUITY

You feel a stir of excitement. Magic and old things always fascinate you. "I'm surprised to find such a shop in this dumb town," you tell Rynath.

"All the more likely in an out-of-the-way village," Rynath replies.

"Do we dare go in?"

"I don't think anyone in these parts will recognize you, especially the way you look now," says the elf. "Just don't give yourself away!" Then she adds, chuckling, "Perhaps you can purchase a new web-casting spell. Your old web spell somehow managed to tangle the entire second floor of the castle for hours in that sticky goop."

You flush with anger at Rynath's kidding as she adds, "And maybe you can buy a spell to get back that purse of money you lost along the way. Money will be scarce till we get more from home."

You bring the unpleasant conversation to a sudden close by pushing past the smiling elf into the bookery.

"Good morrow, young gentleman," says a tall, elderly woman from behind a rack of scrolls. She wears a long emerald-green gown with a wide brown sash. "Perhaps I can interest you in a spell to solve your problems," she says mysteriously.

You feel your face begin to redden again. "Now even total strangers are making fun of me!" you exclaim, whirling around to leave.

"No one is making fun of you," Madam Ursula calls after you. "As a matter of fact, many people solve their problems at my bookery."

Your curiosity aroused, you pause and examine the woman more closely in the dim, musty bookery. "What possible information of value could I expect to find in this out-of-the-way town?" you ask skeptically.

"Do not insult knowledge if you wish to dance with it," Rynath says from behind you.

"Wisdom may wear strange clothes," Madam Ursula adds without missing a beat. Far from being angry, she looks at you with a kindly gaze.

This dusty book shop is certainly the last place you would have looked to solve your problems. But somehow you feel that it's all right—short of revealing yourself—to confide in Madam Ursula. You wonder what Rynath will say, but she keeps silent as you speak.

"I don't know if you're aware of all the details of our country's problems. But they are serious, and I want to help. Rampillion, the Crimson Wizard, is at this very moment creating an army of magical lava warriors to attack the royal capital of Balshad. Meanwhile, his army of orcs and humans from Zor is invading Grendopolan's southern border."

Madam Ursula nods slowly. "And how would you solve Grendopolan's problems?" she asks.

"Three centuries ago, Rampillion caused all the dragons to disappear, then vanished himself. Now that the Crimson Wizard has returned to menace Grendopolan once more, I'd like to summon forth a dragon. A number of them were formerly our allies."

A slow, faint smile spreads across Madam Ursula's face as she listens to your explanation. "What if the dragon were to help Rampillion instead?" she asks pointedly.

"Not all dragons are evil," you insist. "If I could conjure up a friendly dragon, I'm sure it would prove to be a great help against the evil Rampillion."

"A daring plan, your high—ah, my young friend," the old woman says, catching her slip in midsentence.

Rynath's hand flashes to the hilt of her sword in alarm. No one is supposed to know who you are. Have you given yourself away somehow?

"Perhaps King Airon and Queen Niade are

too preoccupied with the immediate threat of war to consider a solution such as yours," Madam Ursula says smoothly, glancing quickly at Rynath. Then she turns and approaches an old chest with rusty locks. "I don't show these to many of my customers," she says as she removes something from the chest, "but they may help you find the solution you seek."

Madam Ursula turns back toward you and places a small box on the countertop. Inside, on a velvet cushion, sits a beautiful, ornately carved ring. With a start, you notice that it is shaped like a tiny dragon. "Try it on," Madam Ursula urges you.

You remove the small silver ring from the box and push it onto your finger. The wings of the tiny dragon fit perfectly around your finger. As you admire the ring, you are startled to feel your hand tingle. You feel a surge of power you have never felt before, and you feel strangely excited.

Might this ancient ring somehow strengthen your magical powers? you wonder. You can hardly keep from jumping up and down in expectation.

"This book may prove of interest to you, too, young man," Madam Ursula adds, handing you a heavy leather-bound volume edged with metal.

Still feeling the strange surge of power from the ring, you open the book and silently read the title page:

GRENDOPOLAN MANUAL OF SORCERY FOR SUMMONING AND REPELLING MAJOR DRAGONS

For a moment, you forget all about the ring. After all, you don't know if the ring really has any magical powers. Maybe this strange book could provide a quicker source of help. Maybe it would enable you to summon a dragon to Grendopolan to fight the evil Rampillion.

But you wonder if an apprentice magic-user would have enough control to cast such a spell. Perhaps the ring is your best bet after all. Perhaps it can supply you with the extra strength you know you will need.

And then you remember—you don't have much money to spare.

"How—how much do they cost?" you ask.

"Two hundred crowns each," Madam Ursula answers. "A bargain at twice that price."

Quickly calculating how much you'll need for room and board at the inn till more money arrives, you decide you can buy either the ring or the book—but not both.

1) If you choose to buy the ring to increase your magical powers, turn to page 18.

2) If you decide instead to buy the book so you can summon a dragon to fight Rampillion, turn to page 133.

"We'll never get this close to the prisoners again," you reason aloud. "You're right, Rynath! We've got to try to rescue Erik now! We can't hope to overpower that monster," you go on, pulling out the manual of sorcery from your shoulder pouch and flipping through the pages. "Tell me all you know about the tarantella's power."

Rynath holds Glitteredge ready at her side as she keeps watch for other guards. "The mad dance caused by the bite hypnotizes all who watch it. Then they, too, dance until they die of exhaustion or become too weak to defend themselves against the spider's attack."

"Here's something about warding off the poison of dragons," you say. "Maybe I can alter that spell somehow to use against the tarantella."

An arrow whizzes through the air and slams into the wall behind you. You duck your head and keep reading.

"I think I've found something we can use!" you cry as another volley of arrows shatters against the stone wall nearby. "It's a spell designed to protect its user from a dragon's hypnotic stare!"

Rynath pushes you around the corner of the stairwell, and you stumble to the door leading to the prison cells.

"We've got to get away from here fast! Quick! Through this door and down the steps!" the elf commands as she forces open the lock on the door with her sword.

"We'll be walking straight into the spider's mouth!" you exclaim.

"Then your spell had better work," Rynath replies grimly.

You and Rynath creep into the room and manage to crawl under a jailer's table before the tarantella sees you. You overturn the table to serve as a shield, not only from the arrows but also from the spider, which is now advancing toward you.

Frantically you search for the right words to use in the spell as Rynath hacks at the tarantella with Glitteredge. An arrow, meant for you, thuds into the spider, and in a frenzy of rage, it smashes the table into kindling.

Defenseless now, you stand only a few scant feet before the jaws of the angry creature and chant:

"Let tarantella stare in vain;
  Let magic ward off deadly bite!
  Instead, let our foes dance in pain
  As giant spider leads the fight!"

The tarantella suddenly seems to lose interest in the two of you. As a platoon of orcs rush down the stairs, the hairy monster turns on them!

The spider sinks its stinger into the nearest orcs, who begin a mad dance around the prison chamber. As the other guards watch, one by one they begin to drop their weapons and join in the strange dance.

"Shield your eyes!" you call to the prisoners in the cells.

"The keys are hanging there on the wall!" a voice shouts from one of the cells.

"That sounds like Erik!" you cry. "Erik, it's me, Treon!"

"Treon? How did you get—"

"There's no time to explain that now," you interrupt. "We've got to get out of here as quickly as possible!"

You unlock the cells of the Grendopolan prisoners, who arm themselves with the orcs' fallen swords and axes.

"Good work, Treon!" your older brother says as you head for the stairs leading out of the dungeon. "Now that we're free and armed, I'm sure my men and I can fight our way out of here."

"I don't think that will be necessary, Erik," you say. "Most of the enemy soldiers are too— ah—busy to try to stop you."

Eric looks around the chamber at the dancing orcs, then laughs heartily. "Well, at least let me get you the best horse in the stable. We'll catch up with Calford in no time, and you can watch us make mincemeat out of Rampillion's army!"

"Ah—I don't think that will be necessary, either, Erik," you say calmly as you hear Rynath chuckle. "You see, I already have a ride, and I think I may be seeing Calford long before you do."

You reach the top step and walk out into the

open courtyard. "Erik," you say, looking up, "I want you to meet Ayrsayle."

"Who's Ayr—" your brother starts to say, then stops in midsentence to stare open-mouthed as the sky is suddenly filled with the form of the enormous golden dragon.

"Ayrsayle's just a new friend I happened to meet along the way," you say with a grin.

THE END

"I'll buy the ring," you tell Madam Ursula as you feel another surge of power pulse through your body. Quickly you count out the coins. If the Zorians or the lava warriors manage to break through the royal army's defenses, you will have a weapon to use immediately.

"The dragon ring fits only people of rare quality, my young friend," the old woman says mysteriously.

You flip through the pages of the sorcery manual one last time, wondering if you have made the right choice.

"Would you like to borrow the book tonight and return it to me in the morning? I'm sure I can trust you."

You look at Rynath, who wrinkles her pale forehead quizzically. "You show great trust in total strangers, madam," she says dubiously

"Your friend now possesses the dragon ring," Madam Ursula replies. "I am certain that, one way or another, he shall meet his obligations."

The old woman's confident manner only seems to bother Rynath more, but finally, grudgingly, she allows you to borrow the book.

On the way back to your inn, the Rising Phoenix, the elf says suspiciously, "I'd swear she knew who you were when we walked in. At least she does now."

"If you felt I was in danger, why did you let me go on about our country's problems?"

For once the elf is silent. After a long pause,

she continues. "Why did the old woman call the book a manual? It's merely a collection of stories about dragons called, *Famous Dragons From Grendopolan's Past.*"

You knit your brow thoughtfully but say nothing. You don't understand this remark at first, but gradually an idea forms in your mind. Can it be that the true contents of the book are only visible to those destined to use it? It seems too incredible to believe, yet somehow. . . .

Your thoughts are temporarily interrupted by your arrival at the Rising Phoenix. Rynath escorts you to your room. At the door, she says, "I'll check on the latest reports from Balshad and the Zorian border. At the same time, I'll see if more money has arrived. Try not to cast any unfortunate spells from your storybook until I return," she adds with a grin.

Practically shutting the door in her face, you turn to settle down with the borrowed book. You open the heavy, yellowed volume to the title page. " 'Grendopolan Manual of Sorcery . . .' " you read aloud, your mind recalling Rynath's apparent inability to see the real title.

Perhaps the book has had a protection spell placed on it. That would allow only a wizard to read the true title of the book. You recall Madam Ursula's words about the ring fitting "only people of rare quality." Perhaps that's what she meant, you think with a burst of excitement.

Soon you find yourself deep in explanations of ancient spells and tales of strange, powerful dragons from Grendopolan's fascinating past. As you turn a page, you see a picture of a dragon that somehow looks familiar—the dragon of your ring!

You read the story of Ayrsayle, guardian dragon of the magic portals of Grendopolan. It tells of how Rampillion used a transformation spell to imprison Ayrsayle within a ring. Could this be the very ring?

Fascinated, you read on, skimming past passages that tell of another great dragon, the evil Fyrewhyp. You learn that only another sorcerer, one who understands the ancient ways, can free Ayrsayle by casting a spell.

Perhaps the book contains the wording for such a spell. Growing increasingly excited, you read further and discover what seems to be the spell you are looking for. But—your excitement cools a bit—your sister Daphal and your mother have warned you never to attempt spells beyond your level of experience. Your mind reels as you weigh the risk of casting the spell.

1) If you think you should heed the warning of your mother and sister and not risk uncertain sorcery, turn to page 25.

2) If you choose to ignore their warning and try to free Ayrsayle with a spell, turn to page 46.

Once more you remember Rynath's words of wisdom during one of your chess lessons. "Never toy with a dangerous opponent, particularly one who might use your carelessness against you at a later time."

You hope desperately that your mother, Queen Niade, is able to sustain her magical powers awhile longer to keep Fyrewhyp at bay. "We must checkmate Rampillion now, before he has a chance to recover," you declare to Daphal and Rynath.

"A strange choice of words, Treon, but somehow appropriate," your sister replies. "Rynath, if Treon distracts the Crimson Wizard, do you think you can sneak up behind him without being noticed?"

"I think so," Rynath replies, "but I don't think I could overpower him. I'm sure he must have spells available to defend himself in case of personal attack."

Daphal shakes her head. "While I was held captive, I discovered that Rampillion's magical staff gives him power over the lava warriors. You need only to get his staff away from him, not overpower him. I think I can formulate a spell that will force him to drop it for a few seconds."

Rynath squirms out of the vine ropes and scrambles up the slope among the cover of the boulders. Meanwhile, you fly to the other side of the forest and land beyond sight of the volcano. "It is imperative that you keep Rampillion busy, if we are to succeed," Daphal says.

Your sister wrinkles her brow and concentrates hard as she chants a spell. Finally she says, "My detect magic spell indicates Rampillion has taken cover behind three boulders on the edge of the clearing by the sealed tunnel entrance."

You rise high into the air, spot the three boulders, circle the clearing, and dive straight at the boulders, breathing fire. Rampillion is too busy warding off your blasts to hurl any spells of his own.

As the ring of flames around the sorcerer starts to flicker out, Daphal casts a spell, and suddenly Rampillion's staff glows white hot. He screams in pain and drops it.

Immediately you dive at him, claws extended and fangs bared. Despite the absence of his magical staff, Rampillion nevertheless hurls a repelling spell that is strong enough to knock you out of the sky.

As you regain control and swoop to a shaky landing, you notice that Rynath has crept through the tall grass in the confusion. Reaching between two rocks, she grabs the staff and retreats among the boulders. Without his staff, the Crimson Wizard loses control of the weird lava warriors, and they turn on him ruthlessly.

The last you see of them, the rock creatures are marching up the slope of the volcano and jumping in. A scream breaks off abruptly as the last of the creatures jumps into Enam holding onto the Crimson Wizard. The evil glowing monsters have returned from whence they came, taking their creator along with them.

Soon you recover from your near crash landing and discover that you are relatively unharmed. Now you can unite your magical powers with those of Daphal and your mother to defeat Fyrewhyp. As you fly off with Daphal and Rynath on your back, you wonder if you'll ever regain human form—or if you'll live your life as a dragon all the way to . . .

THE END

"I am, after all, only an apprentice wizard," you think. "I shouldn't compose a dangerous spell without help."

You remember how your brother Erik teased you into showing off and making a sprite appear on the banquet table at your parents' anniversary celebration. They were far from pleased to have slept right through the feast held in their honor, you recall ruefully.

Turning back to the dragon manual, you read the history of Fyrewhyp, a huge red dragon who burned several villages in Grendopolan and killed everyone who tried to defend them. Finally the Emerald Wizard, Jalquin, a remote ancestor of yours, trapped Fyrewhyp inside Mount Enam, one of the five mountains that ring the city of Balshad.

Toward the end of the chapter, you come upon a spell that is supposed to summon Fyrewhyp. You think it's odd, since there was no spell to call forth Ayrsayle. But the spell looks legitimate enough.

Through the window, you see Rynath returning to the Rising Phoenix. You decide to put the book aside, but first you read the spell for calling Fyrewhyp. Without thinking, you find yourself giving voice to the words.

Please turn to page 46.

"I've made too many mistakes with sorcery already," you tell the talking ring. "I'm going to hope my elf friend Rynath comes to rescue me."

"Could you at least recite a counterspell to free me from your finger?" Ayrsayle asks. "With such a spell, I would not change size, but at least I could escape from this place."

You see no harm in the tiny dragon's request, so you concentrate for a few moments, then chant:

"Let tiny dragon be set free;
  Regain your wings and from here flee!"

You feel a shock pulse through your finger, then Ayrsayle disappears with a puff of smoke and a small POP! You see what looks like a tiny butterfly circling above your head, but you know it's actually Ayrsayle.

You look down at your bare finger.

"I'm sorry you're so cautious, human," the tiny dragon says, hovering above your head. "Good luck with Rampillion!" You watch as the tiny Ayrsayle flutters out the tower window.

You hear a key turn in the lock, and two orcs in chain mail fling open the door. Behind them stands a tall, bearded figure in bright red wizard's robes.

"So you were able to free Ayrsayle," Rampillion says, noticing your bare finger. "Talented work for an inexperienced apprentice."

The two orc guards quickly chain your arms and legs together as the evil wizard goes on: "However, I can still use your royal wizard's power to help me keep control of the portals. I'll just have to wear YOU on my finger instead of that meddling dragon!" he says with a laugh.

Then Rampillion opens a vial of bubbling potion and pours it over your head as he chants a spell in the ancient dragon language.

You feel your arms and legs pulling around and touching each other behind your back. Your chains fall away as you feel your body shrinking.

"A fine new ring to add to my collection!" the Crimson Wizard chortles in approval as he picks you up and puts you on his finger. "Now, on to the magic portals! Nothing can stop my army from overrunning Grendopolan now!"

THE END

"I can't help!" you cry. "I'm not even sure how the magic in the book works. I—I might just make things worse!"

The golden dragon looks you straight in the eye, shakes her mighty head sadly, then flies off toward the burning town. You follow as fast as you can, running down a lane to the edge of town, with Rynath dashing along behind you. The two dragons at first circle each other tentatively, then suddenly the battle is on! You hear great booming sounds like a gigantic thunderstorm. Bolts of flame light up the sky, and through it all the air is filled with the roar of terrible challenges.

"Look!" you shout to Rynath. "Ayrsayle seems to be outmaneuvering Fyrewhyp. She seems too quick for him!"

Rynath shakes her head. "But the red dragon's flame is more powerful. I fear the golden dragon cannot evade its fiery blasts for long. Look now! The gold dragon's wing has been burned!"

"I'm sure I wouldn't have been able to help with one of my spells," you mumble miserably, feeling guilty.

With no one to come to her aid, the mighty Ayrsayle is soon seriously crippled by Fyrewhyp's fiery breath. Unable to manuever, she can no longer avoid Fyrewhyp's slashing claws and cruel fangs. In a few short moments, only one dragon—a red one—remains in the sky over the town.

You turn and dash down the country lane,

watching over your shoulder as Fyrewhyp sets fire to the rest of Trigedium.

"I . . . hope . . . we're able to outrun those flames," you stammer between gasps for breath.

"Dragons fly faster than we can ever hope to run," Rynath reminds you, her face filled with fear.

Suddenly a gigantic shadow blots out the sun. Turning, you see Fyrewhyp swooping down upon you, and you realize with a sinking feeling that this is surely . . .

THE END

You must find some way to free Daphal. You reread the chapter about Fyrewhyp in the dragon manual, then return the book to your shoulder pouch. Carefully you choose the words to cast an ancient spell you only half understand. You feel your ring finger begin to tingle. Then the tingle increases to a pulsing throb as you chant aloud:

"Correct the errors of my tongue;
Let dragon ring now come to life.
Arise from sleep where you have hung.
Protect the realm from Fyrewhyp's strife!"

You brace yourself for the familiar spinning sensation as Rynath covers her eyes. The supernatural storm swirls around you with breathtaking force. You feel a burning deep in your throat, and your shoulder blades begin to itch furiously. Then a clap of thunder knocks you senseless.

You come to, wondering how many times you have lost consciousness in a single day.

Slowly you stretch your wings and sigh a breath of fire into the air.

Wings? Fire?

Your eyes dart up and down your body in one quick movement. You see a light gold stomach, deep golden scales, and a long, graceful tail. . . . There's no escaping it. You have a dragon's body!

You take a deep breath and cough. Three tall trees nearby go up in flames.

Suddenly you feel something like a mosquito bite on your left foot. Peering far below you, you see a tiny Rynath raising her sword to swing a second time.

"What have you done with my human friend, foul dragon?" Rynath shouts fearlessly. "Return him at once, or you will feel my elven blade once more!"

"Maybe someday I'll learn to make magic spells come out exactly the way I want them to," you sigh, your voice booming like a dozen bass drums.

Rynath pauses in midswing and stares at you, her eyes wide with surprise. "Treon?" the elf asks uncertainly.

"How else would I know that your sword is called Glitteredge," you ask, "or that you received the scar on your left arm when you grew careless while trying to teach me two-handed sword fighting?"

Rynath lowers her sword slowly as the truth sinks in. "I must say, I like our odds against the lava warriors much better now than I did before. Do you think you can handle that huge body?"

"I doubt it," you reply. "But we don't have much choice. Climb up on my back."

Not knowing what to expect, you make your first awkward takeoff, skimming the top from a small tree with one wing. Once airborne, however, you begin to feel increasing confidence. You begin to reexamine the options your new, powerful form makes possible.

Daphal or Fyrewhyp? You should be able to rescue your sister easily now, but if you do, the dragon might do considerable damage in the meantime. If you go after Fyrewhyp, you can at least even the score.

1) If you decide to rescue Daphal first, then go after Fyrewhyp, turn to page 136.

2) If you decide to fight Fyrewhyp immediately, turn to page 119.

Rynath grabs a branch from the campfire to use as a torch, and as the royal warriors prepare to defend themselves against the charging orcs, you race toward the cave.

Huddled inside the cave, you say to Rynath, "Do you think my counterspell that freed the dragon from the ring might have broken all of Madam Ursula's other transformation spells, too?"

"Yes, I suppose that's possible, but I'm no magic-user," Rynath replies, holding the sputtering torch close to the spell book as you search its pages. "Why do you ask?"

"Here it is, right here in the chapter on reversing spells!" you say excitedly. " 'If a wizard breaks another sorcerer's spell, it is sometimes possible to use the original magic himself if he rewords it correctly.' "

"It's a dangerous plan, my prince!" the elf replies, frowning.

Outside the cave, the clanging of swords sounds dangerously close.

A mace whistles through the air into the cave, knocking the manual of sorcery from your hands. A pair of orcs, clad in black armor and wielding battle-axes, have spotted Rynath's torch!

"Reword the spell quickly, Treon!" Rynath yells as she draws Glitteredge. "We don't have any choice!"

The first monster charges into the cave. Rynath throws the torch in its face, then parries the thrust of its weapon with her sword.

Fortunately you have read all you need to cast the spell. You quickly form the words:

"Tiny dragon is now well;
Ursula's power shrinks away.
To right her wrongs, I take her spell
And use her magic in this fray."

The second orc enters the cave, forces its way past Rynath and the first orc, and stands over you, its battle-ax raised high.

You cross your hands in the air to finish the spell, and your ring finger burns like a fiery ember. Suddenly the orcs simply disappear!

Rynath breathes a sigh of relief and retrieves the torch. Then she stoops over and picks up something from the ground. "Treon, this proves you are no longer merely an apprentice wizard!" she says in awe.

She holds up two tiny rings. As you examine them, you see two leering orc faces looking back up at you. The spell worked!

You and Rynath find Calford on the field of battle and explain quickly what you have done. "If you were able to transform the Zorian general and the orc chief, too, the rest of the invaders might give up," your brother shouts over the din of battle.

You adjust the spell once more and hurl it again, this time across the battle lines.

Screams of surprise and alarm from the enemy camp tell you the sorcery has worked. Calford bellows a warning of your power as a wizard and throws the two orc rings across to the enemy as further proof. Soon the air is filled with the sound of the invaders fleeing through the desert.

After a short rest, the royal army begins its victorious march back to Balshad.

"Well, Treon," your brother says, "it looks as if you're going to make it as a real wizard after all."

You pat your dragon manual, safe in your shoulder pouch. "Thanks to a certain book about dragons, Calford," you reply with a broad grin.

THE END

"You're right, Rynath," you admit. "Much as I hate to say it, the safety of an entire city is more important than Daphal. Come on!"

You scramble down the mountain as fast as you can. Twice you are forced to duck for cover to avoid patrols of lava warriors.

A mile down the slope, a tongue of red fire licks over the rim of Mount Enam. Then you see the flame again, this time hundreds of feet above Enam, and realize it's not the volcano. It's Fyrewhyp!

The huge red dragon circles the city, then dives from the sky with a terrible roar. It heads straight for Balshad's northern watchtower, the highest point of the city.

Lookouts shoot arrows at the beast, but they bounce harmlessly off its tough hide. Extending its menacing claws, the dragon snaps off the top of the tower as a small child would topple a pile of blocks.

As you watch in horror, Fyrewhyp rises above the city to renew the attack.

"Hundreds of people will be killed," you say miserably, "and all because of me!"

But as the evil dragon plummets toward the castle again, you see eerie waves of emerald rings suddenly surround the watchtower.

"It's my mother's sorcery!" you cry in relief. "She's cast a magic shield around the castle!"

The dragon's claws cannot penetrate the shield. Its flaming breath bounces off harmlessly, failing to singe even an eyelash of the cheering archers below.

"My mother's magical strength must be drained from repelling the lava warriors," you say worriedly. "This will only tire her more. Since we're too late to warn her about Fyrewhyp, we've got to free Daphal so she can use her magic to help Mother."

"And march right into the arms of the lava monsters?" Rynath asks, horrified. "How can we hope to rescue your sister?"

"We'll think of something," you say, hoping you are right.

Please turn to page 31.

"We must return to Balshad," you decide. "Mother is an experienced magic-user, and she'll know how best to use my dragon body to defeat Fyrewhyp."

Daphal and Rynath mount your powerful shoulders and crawl onto your neck. You manage a considerably smoother takeoff this time, and in just a few short moments, you are circling the royal castle.

"Look at that huge break in the northern wall!" your sister shouts.

"At least Fyrewhyp isn't anywhere in sight. Queen Niade must have been able to drive off the red dragon for the time being," Rynath says as she scans the sky.

You land a safe distance from the castle walls so as not to cause the archers undue concern. Daphal climbs from your neck and hurries into the castle. Soon you see your sister return with your mother, who stares at you in astonishment.

"I welcome all reinforcements at this point . . . uh . . . Treon," the queen says, "but how came you by your present form?"

You review the strange sequence of events in your mind, then explain as clearly as you can how you summoned Fyrewhyp by mistake, then transformed yourself into a dragon.

"Legend has it that Fyrewhyp is an accomplished, ferocious fighter," your mother comments as she inspects your scaly golden body. "After warding off the evil dragon this afternoon, I think I must agree with the legends.

However bravely you fight, Fyrewhyp's experience must surely defeat you."

"What do you suggest I do, Mother?" you ask.

"Daphal and I could merge our magical powers to cast an invisibility spell on you," your mother replies. "Both our powers have been badly drained today, but together we should be able to keep you from being seen for the entire battle."

"But—but that's not fair!" you protest.

"Do not be bothered by that, Treon," your mother reassures you. "Fyrewhyp is an extremely experienced fighter. Even an invisible opponent may prove no match for it. This will only help to even the odds."

"The red dragon approaches!" cries a soldier from the lookout tower.

"You must be ruthless, Treon," Daphal shouts. "Only surprise and determination will save our family and loyal subjects!"

With Daphal's help, Queen Niade utters the words of the invisibility spell, and slowly you fade from view. Taking the air and arching your huge unseen body high above Fyrewhyp, you dive for your unsuspecting foe, scoring a hit on the red dragon's neck with your first slashing attack.

But when you renew the attack, Fyrewhyp instinctively lashes out into the air with its claws, belching a stream of dragonfire in all directions.

"Mother was right," you think. Fyrewhyp

can still hear the beat of your wings, even if the red dragon can't see you.

Your inexperience in flying and fighting almost enables the red dragon to slay you several times. Only your invisibility protects you from a fatal death grip.

Finally you summon all your courage and pounce on Fyrewhyp's back. You lock your legs securely around the huge body and try to protect yourself with your wings against the red dragon's slashing claws. After several long moments, you feel Fyrewhyp's struggling begin to weaken, and the next thing you know you are both falling through the sky toward the ground below.

You tear yourself free from its final clutching grip only moments before Fyrewhyp crashes to the ground. Shaking with fear and weakened from the battle, you glide to the outer wall of the castle. At that moment, your body blinks into sight as the invisibility spell wears off.

"Neither of your brothers has ever battled with more courage!" your mother tells you proudly after you land. "But we have no time to lose," she adds. "Some transformation spells can become permanent if they last too long. We must change you back into your human form as soon as possible!"

"But we still have to face Rampillion!" you cry. "My dragon body may prove useful against Rampillion's powerful magic."

"That is true, Treon," your mother says with

a sigh. "I'm afraid the choice must be up to you."

1) If you decide to try to regain your human form now, turn to page 145.

2) If you decide to remain a dragon long enough to fight Rampillion and take a chance on remaining a dragon forever, turn to page 101.

"I doubt if the dragon sorcery manual would have any spells to stop a live volcano," you say. "If Rampillion started this eruption with his magic, he must be the one to stop it."

You fly into a thick cloud of ashes, cinders, and blinding smoke. You and Rynath begin to cough uncontrollably and rub your stinging eyes. Ayrsayle dives quickly and emerges below the smoke, almost level with the mountain range.

But now your enemies have spotted you. Lava warriors on the slope below point up at you and shake their huge fists. You see Rampillion raising his arms to cast a spell, then suddenly he blinks out of sight.

"He's cast an invisibility spell!" Rynath cries. "He'll escape if we don't capture him right away. We've got to land and go after him on foot!"

"But without Ayrsayle to protect us, we'll be at the mercy of the lava warriors!" you cry. "And more of them are pouring out of the volcano every minute! They're sure to march on Balshad soon!"

1) If you decide to remain with Ayrsayle to stop the lava warriors, even though you know the Crimson Wizard is sure to escape if you do, turn to page 116.

2) If you choose to leave the protection of the gold dragon to try to capture Rampillion, choose page 141.

" 'It burns the land from north to south
Of all who dare its flaming lip.
Beware the lightning of the mouth
And the snaking tail of Fyrewhyp,' "

you read aloud from the book.

Before the last word is out of your mouth, a terrible wind blasts open the door to your room with a loud crash. You hear it howl eerily through the corridors of the Rising Phoenix.

"What have I done?" you shout as you clutch the book tightly to your chest and run outside.

Lightning crackles through the darkened sky all around you. You look up and see, not lightning, but a real-life Fyrewhyp swooping straight toward you, flames shooting out of its mouth. You've got to decide what to do quickly, or it will be too late!

1) If you decide to run for your life, turn to page 67.

2) If you choose to try to find a counter-spell to use against Fyrewhyp, turn to page 98.

"There aren't enough lava warriors left to launch an attack on Balshad now that most of them are trapped inside the tunnel," you reason, "and Rampillion certainly won't try to attack singlehanded. It was I who released Fyrewhyp through my blundering. Now I've got to protect the city from further harm," you decide.

"All right, if you must, Treon. I won't argue with your decision," Daphal replies. "But I still think Rampillion presents our biggest danger. Leave me here, and I'll keep track of him until you return."

"Remember how dangerous he is," Rynath warns.

As you glide to a landing on one of the lower slopes of the volcano, Daphal pats the elf's arm reassuringly. "You two have already rescued me once today. I'll make sure you shan't have to do it again."

Daphal jumps off your back and continues. "When the Crimson Wizard stops and I can risk trying a mind link with Mother, I'll let you know his location," she says as you spread your wings. "And you be careful, too. Remember, you still have a human mind inside that dragon's body, but Fyrewhyp has been using its body a great deal longer!"

You soar high into the clouds to survey the situation near the city. Although the wall of the castle is flaming brightly and many brave royal warriors lie still on the battlements, you see that your mother's sorcery has succeeded in injuring the great red dragon. Its left wing is bent and crippled, and its fiery breath does not seem nearly as strong as it was when you last saw it.

Even so, you are new at fighting with claws, fangs, and dragonfire. You feel your best bet is to take whatever advantage of Fyrewhyp's exhaustion you can. Diving at the great dragon repeatedly, you strike glancing blows, then fly out of reach. After half an hour of this, you have suffered only minor cuts, but the red dragon seems seriously injured and can scarcely remain airborne.

"Your mother is signaling from the castle watchtower," Rynath says. "It looks as if the queen wants you to pick her up. She must have recognized me."

You examine your deadly opponent. Although obviously wounded and tired, Fyrewhyp is still crafty. The red dragon might pretend weakness, then attack when your back is turned.

You wait until you have once more raked the red dragon with your claws and it has flown off to a safe distance to try to recover. Then you race toward the royal castle. Queen Niade stands alone on the battlements, leaning wearily on her wizard's staff. Gently you scoop her up in your front claws, then soar skyward once more.

Quickly Rynath's explains how you came to be transformed into a dragon. "Perhaps you've finally discovered your calling, Treon," you mother says as the wind rushes by your face. "We certainly have never had a dragon in our family before!"

Just then a stream of flame just misses your head, and you look up to see Fyrewhyp diving straight toward you, looking somewhat refreshed. You tuck your wings and roll to the side. The great red beast slashes the tip of your tail with its fangs.

"Fyrewhyp has not been defeated yet!" Rynath cries.

"Lure him over the mouth of Mount Enam, Treon," your mother says. "Leave the rest to me."

You plunge for the crater of the volcano, feeling Fyrewhyp's flaming breath right behind you.

You fly straight into the fiery jaws of the crater, Fyrewhyp at your tail. At the last possible moment before you plunge into the boiling lava, you swerve straight up, narrowly clearing the wall of the crater. Your move catches Fyrewhyp by surprise. The red dragon tries to swerve upward, but before it can clear the top of the volcano, your mother casts a wizard lock spell. Fyrewhyp is trapped inside the Enam Volcano!

Your joy is short-lived as you remember Rampillion. You still must face him, and he might prove to be the more dangerous foe. Still, you have defeated one of your two enemies using your new dragon powers. Only one more to go!

As you fly back toward Balshad, you plan your next move.

1) If you feel confident enough of your new abilities to go after Rampillion on your own, turn to page 102.

2) If you decide to remain in Balshad until you have heard from Daphal, then go after Rampillion with your rested mother along to help, turn to page 110.

You emerge safely from the magic portal and find yourselves high in the sky over the Zorian border. After half an hour of flying over desert country, you spot several soldiers bearing the royal standards of Grendopolan. You recognize one of them, Larpak, as a trusted officer and close friend of your brother Erik. The men are obviously fatigued from battle, and several of their uniforms are blood-stained from injuries.

The warriors leap back in terror as the dragon descends and lands in their midst. Finally Larpak recognizes you. "Prince Treon, is the beast friendly?" he asks, raising his broadsword tentatively.

"You needn't fear the dragon, Larpak," you tell him. "Ayrsayle is our new ally. How goes the battle?"

"The Zorian army has broken through our lines," the knight explains wearily. "Even now your brother Calford is attacking the enemy's flank with the royal cavalry as they march toward Balshad."

"What about my brother Erik?" you ask with concern.

Larpak hangs his head. "An orc stunned Erik with a rock during the fighting. They've taken him and many other prisoners to the Zorian dungeon at Lerthune."

"Should we go to the aid of Calford in his attack against the invading army?" Rynath asks you as Ayrsayle readies her wings to fly.

"Or should we try to rescue Erik from the

dungeon?" you reply, echoing your tutor's thoughts.

1) If you decide to help Calford, turn to page 95.

2) If you go to rescue Erik, choose page 123.

You are too frightened by what has happened to dare to try a new spell to summon Ayrsayle. Something might go wrong again. Your tongue feels frozen, but your finger is still on the page in the dragon book containing the spell that summoned Fyrewhyp. You force yourself to concentrate on rewording the original spell that set the evil dragon free.

The red dragon plummets toward the burning inn, readying its dragonfire for the kill.

"Run, Treon!" Rynath shouts, trying to push you out of the way.

"I can't!" you scream back. Fyrewhyp's bloodred wings fill the sky. The gigantic dragon opens its jaws, and as the bright orange flame blazes forth, you close your eyes, and gathering all your courage, you chant:

> "Protect my home, my land, and me
> From lightning breath of Fyrewhyp.
> Remove this monster instantly;
> Send dragon back on homeward trip."

Suddenly you hear a strange crackling sound in the air all around you, and the wind howls fiercely about you. You stand unmoving, awaiting the fiery blast you are certain must come.

After several seconds, you risk opening one eyelid. To your relief, you see no dragonfire in the sky. In fact, you see no dragon. Fyrewhyp has disappeared! Only the fierce, mysterious wind remains.

Before you have time to congratulate yourself, the howling whirlwind sucks you and
Rynath into freezing blackness. Your ring finger tingles uncontrollably, and wind and
thunder crash about you in total darkness
until you feel everything go black.

You wake to discover yourself on a moun-
taintop. Stuffing the dragon book into your
shoulder pouch, you look around curiously.
You see several familiar-looking peaks, then
the unmistakable glow of the Enam Volcano
rising high above you.

With a shock, you realize you are just outside Balshad, hundreds of miles from where
you were just moments before.

Nearby, Rynath rubs her head and heaves a
sigh. "That was some spell for an apprentice
wizard, Treon!" she says. "What happened?"

Confused, you shake your head and say, "I
don't know . . . unless . . . that must be it! The
sorcery manual says that my ring is a real
dragon trapped by Rampillion. The counterspell must have worked on BOTH dragons! It
returned us to our home. . . ."

"But what happened to Fyrewhyp?" the elf
asks.

You have a terrible thought. "Fyrewhyp's
home is Mount Enam. I've saved Trigedium,
but I've transported that evil dragon practically outside the gates of the royal capital! We
must warn my parents about the danger!" you
tell Rynath. "Fyrewhyp could attack the city
at any moment! That's just the advantage

those lava warriors would need to storm the castle!"

The two of you hurry down the gravelly mountain slope, crashing your way through tangled underbrush and stumbling over jagged rocks. Suddenly Rynath jerks you down quickly and jams your head into the yellow torch grass.

"Something's coming over the rise," she hisses, reaching for her sword.

Peering through the high grass, you see several creatures of molten lava, carrying heavy war spears and maces, moving among the pine trees. Their dark red hide gives off a dull, eerie glow. Two of the monsters force a resisting human along between them. As they pass less than twenty paces from your place of hiding, you suddenly recognize the prisoner.

"It's my sister Daphal!" you whisper in shock.

"She must have been scouting the lava creatures when she was captured," Rynath theorizes.

Although Daphal's arms are bound behind her with heavy rope, her face is cool and unafraid.

"I wonder why doesn't she cast a spell to free herself," Rynath whispers.

"She must have spent too much of her magical energy trying to avoid capture," you guess. "She doesn't have her magical staff, and she can't move her hands to perform a spell. Both those things would weaken her power, too.

We've got to rescue her before they take her back to the enemy camp." You start to crawl forward cautiously.

"Wait!" The elf grabs you. "What about Fyrewhyp? Unless we warn them, your parents and everyone else in Balshad will be caught totally unprepared!"

1) If you think you must free your sorcerer sister immediately and hope there is still time to warn Balshad of the danger, turn to page 150.

2) If you think you must warn your parents and the people of Balshad first, hoping to rescue your sister later, turn to page 38.

"If my idea works it shouldn't take long," you say to Calford. "Ayrsayle, wait here a few minutes before you leave for Balshad. I'd rather not split up our forces, but if my idea doesn't work, then you can go on alone while we try something else."

You beckon Calford to follow you. Using the cover of the sand dunes, you make your way stealthily toward a large column of orcs and Zorians marching toward Balshad.

When you reach the last dune that conceals you from the advancing column, you whisper, "Keep down, Calford, but be ready to run if this doesn't work!"

You know the spell you are about to try is beyond your ability as an apprentice, but it's got to be tried, whatever the danger. You creep to the top of the dune, then leap to your feet, in plain sight of the startled enemy soldiers, and chant:

"Rampillion's hordes, depart from here.
Let orcs and Zorians flee in fear!"

As far as you can see, enemy soldiers drop their weapons where they stand. Then you hear shouting everywhere: "We're doomed!" "Outta my way! It's every man for himself!" "Run for your lives!"

All about you, fear-crazed troops begin running frantically back toward the Zorian border. Their forms are disappearing over a distant dune as your brother comes up beside you. "Well done, Treon! And you didn't even need Ayrsayle's help!"

You flush crimson as a warm glow passes through your entire body. "And now, on to Balshad!"

Please turn to page 78.

"If the guards capture us, we can't rescue anyone," you decide, racing back up the stairs with Rynath close behind. When you reach the top, you discover two armed orcs blocking your path.

"It's the intruders!" you hear one guard yell as he hurls a mace that narrowly misses your head.

"Run for it!" you shout to Rynath. In your mind, you send out an urgent message to Ayrsayle as you dash down the hallway past an open window.

You round a corner to see a pack of howling rock baboons cutting off your escape. The huge apemen wave their arms, snap their sharp fangs, and rush toward you.

You double back around the corner, only to come face-to-face with the two orcs. Rynath draws Glitteredge and goes after the larger one. You grab a torch from a nearby wall bracket and try to defend yourself against the other orc.

Suddenly the entire outside wall of the dungeon crumbles before your very eyes, and you see the gigantic shape of Ayrsayle! A jet of flame flashes over your head. The orcs and baboons take one look at the massive gold dragon and flee for their lives.

You and Rynath climb on top of Ayrsayle's back and soar up into the sky. As you circle overhead, you see shrieking orcs and howling baboons everywhere.

"We can't help Erik now," Rynath says

regretfully. "Any further attempts would only cause the prisoners' deaths."

You grit your teeth in frustration. "Then we must return to aid Calford. After we defeat the Zorian army, perhaps we can trade prisoners of war for Erik and his men."

Please turn to page 95.

"Queen Niade and my sister Daphal are powerful wizards," you reason aloud. "For the time being, they will be able to defend Balshad from a magical attack. But the royal army is in serious trouble right now. Ayrsayle, take us to the Zorian border!"

Ayrsayle spreads her huge wings, and soon you realize you are flying straight through the invisible portal. Chilled to the bone, you hold tightly to the great dragon's neck as you journey through the blackness of the magic gateway.

What must be mere moments seem like hours, but finally you emerge to find yourselves hovering over the scorching deserts of Zor. As Ayrsayle flies along the Grendopolan border, you see much evidence of great destruction. Several battles rage nearby.

"Look! There's a platoon of Rampillion's orcs!" Rynath cries, pointing.

"They've captured some of our soldiers!" you shout. "They must be taking them back to the dungeons."

"Not for long," Ayrsayle replies. She sweeps back her wings, hangs for an instant in midair, then swoops straight down at the startled orcs, breathing fire and roaring a terrible battle cry.

The orcs flee in panic, leaving their prisoners behind to face what seems to be certain death. Soon you are at the side of the Grendopolan warriors, untying their ropes and reassuring them of their safety.

"The mighty Ayrsayle has returned!" you proclaim triumphantly. "She is here to help us, not harm us."

The men stare at the mighty dragon, who remains motionless. Apparently reassured, one officer finally speaks up.

"The war goes badly, Prince Treon," he reports. You notice that he has a sword wound in his side and limps from another wound to his leg. "Rampillion has reinforced the Zorian army greatly. They broke through your brother Calford's line of defenses and are marching on Balshad!"

"Then we have no time to waste," you shout. "We must catch up with the royal army!"

Please turn to page 95.

Desperately you lunge out of the dragon-fire's path. As you hit the ground, you hear the water in a trough behind you evaporate with an angry hiss. Glancing back, you see the entire first floor of the Rising Phoenix explode into flame. Rynath is nowhere in sight.

"Many thanks for setting me free, feeble human," the red dragon roars down at you.

Leaping to your feet, you run frantically down the street, your pace slowed by the heavy book still clutched to your chest. As you round a corner, you feel your foot slip on a loose cobblestone in the street. The sorcery manual flies from your hands as you instinctively reach out to cushion your fall.

A tongue of fire licks past your head, and a nearby granary erupts into flames. You spring to your feet as an enormous shadow darkens the entire street. You turn to see the dragon almost on top of you now, ready to unleash its fiery flame for the kill. In the nick of time, you remember a trick your brother Erik taught you. Suddenly you tuck your body into a ball and somersault beneath the cone-shaped flame. Feeling intense heat on your back as you rise once more, you rip your smoldering vest from your body and fling it aside.

You feel your finger tingling beneath the dragon ring. Could its magic help you now? But the book's magic brought only bad luck. Maybe if you get rid of the ring, too, your luck will change. Jerking the ring from your finger, you hurl it as far as you can, then look up to see Fyrewhyp circling just above your head.

"Humans are even bigger fools than I thought," the dragon chortles evilly. "You held salvation in your hands and tossed it away."

In a last desperate attempt to escape, you duck down another back street. Your heart sinks in your stomach as you realize it comes to a dead end.

"The book might have helped you, but your second—and last—mistake was getting rid of the ring," the dragon roars. You feel the hot breeze from its flapping wings as the huge creature settles on a nearby roof just above you.

You hear laughter, mingled with the roar of flames from the red dragon's mouth, and as heat like you've never felt before envelops you, you know that this is . . .

THE END

"I never was able to talk any of my children out of something they wanted to do," your mother says ruefully. "But may I at least suggest that you take some help along with you? A human rider could offer guidance if nothing else."

"I've had the most direct experience with the lava creatures. I think I should be the one to go!" Daphal declares, her eyes shining brightly.

"I have spent much of my life looking after the prince's safety, your highness," Rynath says resolutely. "If Treon is determined to fly into danger, it is my responsibility to go with him."

Your mother smiles wanly and nods. "Believe me, faithful Rynath, Treon was getting into plenty of trouble long before you ever became his bodyguard. But your loyalty has earned you a place on this mission. You both shall go."

"Good. What's the plan?" you ask, anxious to get started.

"Treon could attack the lava warriors as they emerge from the secret crevice of the volcano," Daphal suggests. "The creatures won't be prepared, and the battle could be over before it really starts."

"But Treon's powers as a dragon could best be used as the lava soldiers reach Balshad," your mother argues. "The open plains would be much easier to maneuver in than a forest, and the palace guards would be available to help. I suggest that you all remain here with me to present a united front against Rampillion's forces."

1) If you agree with Daphal and think you should fly to the secret crevice to battle the lava warriors as they emerge, turn to page 152.

2) If you think you should remain in Balshad with your mother and the others to present a united front, turn to page 129.

Suddenly you're overcome with anxiety, and you jump up from the rocking chair. "Uh—I just remembered that I have to ask Rynath something!" you say.

You move so quickly that your arm upsets the bottle in Madam Ursula's hand, and the liquid spills all over her. "No, no! Not the transformation potion!" she screams.

The liquid hisses loudly as it makes contact with her skin. A cloud of smoke billows in the air, and the old woman begins to fade before your very eyes.

Screaming, you rush out into the front room of the bookery. Rynath draws her elven blade, Glitteredge, as she glances around the room. "Dive to the floor, Treon!" the elf shouts, hurrying to your side.

You throw yourself to the floor and hear the sound of metal clanging on metal. You look up to see Rynath dueling with an evil-looking orc, which has discarded its gray, hooded cleric's robe.

Two more orcs, also disguised as clerics, reveal themselves now. The shortest pulls out a long, curved dagger.

"Don't kill the prince!" the tallest orc shouts. "We need him alive to help Madam Ursula weave her spells!"

The tall orc lunges at you with its yellow, clawlike hands. Rynath spins away from her opponent, and Glitteredge flashes through the air at your attacker.

As the tall orc ducks under Rynath's blade,

it trips over its long cleric's robe. You grab the thick dragon manual off the counter and bash the creature on the head with it.

But the short orc now blocks the door to the street. The third orc renews its attack on Rynath, slashing at her with its curved blade.

"Run, Treon!" Rynath yells. Glitteredge is a blur of silver as the elf drives back both monsters for a moment. You throw the book at the short orc.

Hoping Madam Ursula isn't waiting for you, you dart into the back room. No one is in sight. You hear the sound of quick footsteps following you, so you hide behind a cabinet filled with old books.

The short orc bursts into the back room with the dragon book under its arm and its dagger held ready. You note that Rynath's blade has brought home at least one wound. A red Zorian army uniform shows through the orc's torn cleric's robe. "What are Rampillion's soldiers doing here in Trigedium?" you wonder.

You look around Madam Ursula's workshop for a weapon but see nothing useful.

Spotting your movement, the yellow-brown monster advances toward you, grating its teeth and snarling, "Surrender now, Prince Treon! You'll save yourself some pain, and maybe we'll even spare your elf friend in there."

You were right not to trust Madam Ursula, and you have no intention of trusting this ugly creature. You roll suddenly underneath a worktable, pushing chairs in front of the advancing orc as you roll. Slowed by the sword wound from Rynath, the orc can't keep up with you.

Then you remember what happened to Madam Ursula only minutes earlier. Removing your gloves from your belt and pulling them on, you grab beakers of hot, bubbling potions from the worktable and hurl them at your enemy.

A large bottle of foul-smelling black liquid strikes the orc. Screaming, the creature throws its arms up as sparks shower the room. A series of flashes explode in brilliant shades of purple and blue, forcing you to shield your eyes.

As the last burst of radiance dies, you look once again and see only a pile of smoldering clothes in a heap on the wooden floor. The orc is gone.

You hear an orc in the front of the bookery groan in pain and fall to the floor, then Rynath pushes open the drapes that separate the back room from the shop.

"Are you all right, Treon?" she asks anxiously. "Where is Madam Ursula?"

You point to a second pile of smoking garments lying by the gently creaking rocking chair. As Rynath bends over the clothes, she says, "It's a sad day when we have to beware of every cleric and shop owner we meet."

Then she rises from the charred remains and says, "It would seem this is a bargain day for jewelry, my prince." She holds out her hand, which has a small object in it. "Let me see your dragon ring again."

You hold up your left hand. Rynath places another ring, similar in style and shape to the dragon ring, on the finger next to it. The band is formed by the arms of the sculpted figure, just as the wings do on the dragon ring. But the figure on the new ring is not a dragon. Instead, the face of Madam Ursula glares up at you, her last look of shock and hatred trapped for eternity in the dark metal of the ring.

After a pause to let Madam Ursula's fate sink in, you tell Rynath about the Zorian uniform the orc was wearing. She tells you that one of the other orcs was wearing the badge and armor of the Crimson Wizard's allies, too.

"Madam Ursula must have been in league with Rampillion," Rynath says. "Obviously she planned to capture you, and this plan must be connected with the other threats to Grendopolan. We know she knew your real identity. She must have needed a royal wizard to somehow help Rampillion overthrow Grendopolan."

"If Madam Ursula could transform people into rings, then maybe she really did come from Sherinad," you say. "And maybe this is a real dragon imprisoned in my ring!" You look down once more at the strange metal band on your finger.

"It's too bad the manual of sorcery was

destroyed when I threw the transformation potion at that orc," you go on, shaking your head. "Now I won't be able to summon the dragon of my ring, if there is one." You stare at Madam Ursula's face in the other ring. "At least Madam Ursula won't be wearing ME around on HER finger. And we've stopped one threat to our country, anyway. Now we have to decide what to do about the Crimson Wizard," you continue.

"Treon, remember that you're supposed to keep out of trouble," your tutor says.

"Yes . . ." you agree slowly, "but trouble seems to find us anyway. We might at least go meet it halfway!"

THE END

As you hover in the sky above Mount Enam, with the gleaming towers of Balshad in sight, you shout, "Look! More lava warriors are crawling out of the volcano! If we go straight to Balshad, it will be like fighting a hydra. For every lava warrior Ayrsayle can destroy, a dozen will appear to take its place.

"Ayrsayle, circle the volcano," you continue. "Somehow we've got to stop this eruption!"

You find it hard to breathe in the scorching air. Even Ayrsayle's dragonfire seems like a candle flame compared to the boiling lava below you.

"What do you suggest, Treon?" Rynath asks.

As you mull over the alternatives, something catches your eye below. "Look! There's a human close to the edge of Enam!"

"It must be Rampillion! And it looks like he's weaving a spell of some sort!" Rynath shouts.

"Rynath, we've got to act now! I could try to use magic to stop Enam's eruption." You hesitate while you think carefully. "Or I might be able to force Rampillion to stop it."

1) If you choose to try sorcery to stop the volcano's eruption, turn to page 127.

2) If you decide to try to make Rampillion himself stop the eruption, turn to page 45.

"We must go to Balshad," you decide. "Rampillion is sure to strike at the capital itself to try to end the war quickly."

Spreading her wings gracefully, Ayrsayle soars into the sky, then plunges through the magic portal in midair. Freezing blackness surrounds you, and for a long moment time and space disappear.

Suddenly you can see again. You see the familiar, mighty royal castle with its tall lookout towers. The five mountains surrounding the capital provide seemingly strong protection against invaders. A trace of smoke curls upward from the peaceful Enam Volcano, and signs of battle are evident outside the great city walls.

"Look below—at the foot of Enam!" Rynath points toward the smoldering volcano. You see a whole troop of lava warriors marching out of a hidden tunnel, heading for Balshad.

As you fly low over the volcano, a fierce rumbling startles you. Immediately you are surrounded by a huge cloud of rising steam. Through it, you see the fiery glow of molten lava below.

Quickly Ayrsayle flaps her mighty wings and soars upward, out of danger.

"This must be Rampillion's sorcery," Rynath shouts over the rumbling. "Enam has been inactive for centuries. The Crimson Wizard must be using the volcano magically to increase his production of lava warriors."

A gust of superheated air tosses Ayrsayle

hundreds of feet higher into the air, almost jarring you loose. You grab for the spiny ridges of the dragon's neck as she struggles to regain her balance. Below, the center of Enam now burns bright red, and a wave of molten lava spills over the rim of the crater.

"We must stop those lava warriors before they reach Balshad!" you say.

"But if Enam erupts, the lava will destroy everything in sight," Rynath argues. "Besides, the volcano spews forth more lava warriors every minute."

While you try to decide what to do next, turn to page 78.

You have no proof that Madam Ursula means you any harm. If you run to Rynath, you may only embarrass yourself and make this kindly old woman feel bad.

You grit your teeth and hold out your injured finger. Madam Ursula carefully pours a small amount of the potion onto the cloth. You see a strange gleam in her eyes as she wraps the cloth around your finger.

Suddenly you begin to feel a burning sensation in your finger. You begin to feel dizzy, and you try to call out to Rynath, but your mouth feels like it's full of cotton, and no sound comes out.

Unable to move, you hear Madam Ursula say, "You will suit my purposes well, young prince. Now I shall finally succeed in conquering Grendopolan—with your help!" And suddenly everything goes black.

You awake, not knowing how much time has passed, with your cheek on a cold stone floor. Rising slowly to your feet, you peer through a small barred window and discover you are in a high tower of a large castle. Beyond the outside castle walls, harsh sand bakes under a searing sun. A single stone pinnacle splits the desert sky.

From stories you've heard, you know you must be in Zor, the land of your country's invaders!

Glancing down, you figure the room you are in is at least two hundred feet above the ground. Your tower cell has only one door, which is bolted and locked. You clutch nervously at your dragon ring. "If only I could fly!" you say bitterly.

"That can be arranged," a small voice replies. You look down at your ring to see the tiny dragon moving its head and looking up at you. You feel dizzy once more, and you shake your head to clear it. "I must be dreaming," you say, "or that magical potion Madam Ursula put on my finger is making me imagine things. Rings don't talk!"

"But dragons do!" the ring says clearly. "We are victims of a common enemy, young prince—the evil Rampillion!"

Questions leap to your mind faster than you can voice them. "Do you mean Madam Ursula is in league with Rampillion? Who are you? And how is it you can speak—"

"Patience, Treon, and you will know everything," the dragon interrupts. "First, Madam Ursula IS Rampillion! And I am Ayrsayle, guardian of the magic portals of Grendopolan before I was imprisoned inside this ring."

"So you ARE really a dragon," you say, the truth finally sinking in. "How did Madam Ursula—I mean Rampillion—trap you?"

"Three hundred years ago, I was the guardian of the magic portals of Grendopolan," Ayrsayle says. "As you may know, a magic portal is a way of getting somewhere else, or sometime else, very quickly, even hundreds of miles away in minutes. Only the guardian of the portals may use them, except that, using very advanced sorcery, a wizard of royal blood could also use the portals in the same way.

"Rampillion imprisoned me in the ring so he could use the magic portals for his own evil purposes," the tiny dragon explains. "He cast a transformation spell on me just as I emerged from a gateway over Balshad, when I was unable to defend myself. By wearing me on his finger, the Crimson Wizard could operate the magic portals even though he is not of royal blood."

"But the plot must have failed," you interrupt. "The portals haven't worked in three centuries—not since my ancestor Jalquin, the Emerald Wizard, disappeared."

"You are related to the brave Jalquin?" the ring asks. "It was he who saved Grendopolan from Rampillion's treachery, Treon. He tried to save me as well just as Rampillion was completing his spell over me."

You hear a door slam at the bottom of the tower, and heavy boots begin mounting the long stairs.

"Then what happened?" you ask hurriedly, wondering who's approaching your cell.

"Jalquin transported himself to the island of Sherinad, the dragon homeland, and told the friendly dragons what Rampillion had done. In the meantime, the Crimson Wizard tried to enlist the evil dragons to his cause. A terrible fight broke out between the good and evil dragons. Finally, rather than risk losing the battle, Rampillion cast a spell that destroyed all of Sherinad. With me on his finger, he escaped through a magic portal to Zor.

"As the island sank into the sea, Jalquin used the last of his magical powers to seal the magic gateways with a hold portal spell," Ayrsayle says.

"And Rampillion vanished from sight until a month ago," you add as the pieces finally begin to fall into place. "But why would the Crimson Wizard want to trap me?"

"Because after centuries of searching, Rampillion finally discovered the spell that unsealed the magic portals. But Rampillion is more cautious after all these years. He wanted a royal wizard to uphold his spell.

"He fears Queen Niade and your sister Daphal too much, so you were the obvious choice."

The footsteps are getting closer, and you can make out the harsh, guttural sounds of orcs.

"But Rampillion has also grown careless," the dragon ring says quickly, hearing the guards approaching. "The magic potion poured on your finger also reversed some of the spell that holds me. If I could only regain my normal size, I could fly us away from here. But I need your help to complete the counterspell."

You have to think quickly. The orcs will soon be at your cell door, and then there will be little time for choices.

Should you aid Ayrsayle in casting a counterspell? What if it backfires, as some of your sorcery has done in the past? You might be squashed by a full-sized dragon in this small tower cell, or you might fall hundreds of feet to the ground. Maybe Rynath has learned what happened and has already launched a rescue party, you think desperately, searching your mind for some measure of hope.

1) If you decide to wait in the hope of being rescued, turn to page 26.

2) If you choose to cast a counterspell to change Ayrsayle to her full size, choose page 105.

"I've got to help," you say quickly. "Ayrsayle wouldn't have asked if she didn't need it!"

You flip frantically through the book of sorcery. "Keep me posted on what's going on," you tell Rynath.

Brilliant trails of flame light up the sky. "The red dragon's fiery breath seems more powerful than Ayrsayle's," Rynath reports, "but Ayrsayle is quicker. So far, the gold dragon has been able to dodge out of the way."

"That's it!" you shout excitedly. "If I can put out Fyrewhyp's dragonfire, Ayrsayle will be able to outfly the red dragon."

"A difficult spell indeed," Rynath protests. "If you make the least miscalculation, you might cast the spell on the wrong dragon. Remember the web spell."

"There's no choice," you snap decisively.

You find the chapter on dragonfire and locate the spell you are looking for. Quickly you chant the words of the spell, then hold your breath and watch, terrified. Suddenly Fyrewhyp's flame is snuffed out in midpuff.

"I did it!" you cry in triumph.

Using her greater quickness, Ayrsayle now dives repeatedly at Fyrewhyp, raking the red dragon's scaly hide with her claws. Her slashing fangs score hit after hit on the slower Fyrewhyp. At last, with a final death cry, the red dragon plummets from the sky, and in a moment you feel the earth shudder from the impact.

"You chose your spell well, Treon," Ayrsayle

tells you as she glides to a landing. "That makes twice you have saved me."

"Then maybe you can help us save Grendopolan," Rynath says eagerly.

"Did you hear news about the fighting?" you ask the elf.

"A messenger arrived just before you started summoning dragons out of thin air," Rynath snorts. "The Zorians have broken through the lines of the royal army, led by your brothers, at Grendopolan's southern border. Rampillion is now launching a full-scale attack on Balshad with his lava warriors."

"And we're stuck here in Trigedium!" you moan.

"Never fear, young wizard," Ayrsayle booms, drawing herself up to her full height. "I will repay my debt, beginning now. Climb on my back. You forget that I am guardian of the magic portals. By entering one, we can be anyplace you want in minutes. But where do you choose to go? Do we go to the aid of your brothers, or do we head straight for Balshad?"

You hadn't thought that far ahead yet, but now you must decide:

1) If you elect to help your brothers fight the Zorian invaders, turn to page 65.

2) If you decide to travel to Balshad to combat the Crimson Wizard and his fierce lava warriors, turn to page 79.

"You've had the chance to judge the danger from the lava warriors firsthand," you say to Daphal. "We must stop the lava warriors before they get to Balshad. We'll just have to hope that Mother can hold off Fyrewhyp until we get there."

"Treon, you may have to do some fancy flying," your sister says. "And if we're thrown off your back, I'll have neither time nor strength to cast a spell to keep us aloft."

"I'll tie us on Treon's back with some of these vines," Rynath says as she stoops to examine the low vines growing everywhere on the slope. Drawing Glitteredge, she cuts through the strong vines and straps Daphal and herself onto your back. With your companions securely in place, you take wing and race toward Mount Enam.

"Rampillion covered the top of the secret crevice with a network of logs, reinforced by magical netting," Daphal explains as you fly. "Then he created a landslide to cover the passage. He's been creating those lava warriors for months under Balshad's very nose!"

"At least now we know his plans," you say as you hover in the sky over Enam. "And the Crimson Wizard certainly won't be expecting me."

"Look!" Rynath cries, pointing below. "Dozens of those molten rock creatures are already marching out of the tunnel!"

"There's not a moment to lose," Daphal says. "Attack whenever you're ready, Treon."

As you dive toward the weird rocklike creatures emerging from the opening below, your
mind reels. "Think ahead," you remember
Rynath telling you over and over again while
she was teaching you chess. "Plan several
moves into the future, and the present will
take care of itself."

Veering suddenly from the lava warriors on
the slope below, you glide instead toward the
opening of the secret crevice. Filling your
huge lungs to capacity, you exhale a stream of
fire straight toward the rubble of rock cover-
ing the tunnel. Again and again you spew
forth your fiery breath, until finally you see
that your plan is working. The very rock cov-
ering the secret tunnel begins to melt, oozing
down to seal off the opening. The lava warriors are sealed inside the tunnel!

You see a tall human figure in scarlet robes,
holding a magical staff and shouting orders to
the lava warriors already outside the tunnel.
Ignoring him, they lumber for cover as you
turn in the air for another dive. The scarlet-
robed figure shakes his fist and utters a curse
at you as he scurries to find protection for himself.

"Rampillion doesn't look too happy," Daphal
says gleefully.

"Look!" Rynath shouts. "More smoke over
the castle! We'd better see how your mother is
faring against Fyrewhyp, or it may be too late
to save the city!"

"But Rampillion knows he has a fire-

breathing dragon on his hands now," you
shout. "Shouldn't we go after him while we've
got him cornered?"

Should you go to the aid of the beleaguered
city, or should you finish off Rampillion while
you have him at a disadvantage? It's up to you
to decide.

1) If you decide to go after Rampillion,
turn to page 21.

2) If, instead, you go to the aid of the city
to battle the red dragon, turn to page
48.

Ayrsayle spreads her wings and soars toward Balshad. As you fly, you see fallen warriors and abandoned weapons scattered everywhere. Although many are orcs and Zorians, some of the motionless figures wear the uniform of the Grendopolan army.

"It looks like our army is doing well so far, but how long can it hold out against such odds?" you sigh. "And how much good can we do against their overwhelming numbers?"

"Foolish apprentice!" Ayrsayle rumbles. "I thought you had read about my race! I am the mighty Ayrsayle, guardian dragon of the magic portals! Rampillion will rue the day he ever plotted against me!"

Soon you hear the sound of horses neighing and swords clanging. Looking down, you see hundreds of mounted warriors, led by your brother Calford. The soldiers are attacking a large army of orcs gathered in a valley. The royal horsemen charge the foot soldiers, then ride off before they can retaliate.

Scanning the battlefield, you spot a separate party of Zorian cavalry circling around behind the royal forces under cover from some low hills. The enemy has almost surrounded Calford's troops!

"Ayrsayle, those Zorians on horseback will—"

"No, they won't, Treon!" the dragon replies crisply. Rynath and you hang on for dear life as the dragon dives headlong toward the enemy.

Ayrsayle's fiery presence causes panic among the Zorian cavalry as her dragon-breath sears the sky. As she swoops low, her great claws hurl rider after rider to the dust, and her enormous wings send horses stamped-ing in every direction.

The Zorian trap foiled, you glide to a land-ing, and your brother crushes you in a tremen-dous bear hug. "Well, Treon, I see you're traveling in style these days! That was a close call just now. Thanks for your help!"

Despite Calford's seemingly cheerful greet-ing, you cannot help but notice the look of exhaustion in his eyes.

"I'd have bet twenty gold pieces we could drive the Zorians back across the border," he goes on in a low voice. "But Rampillion has added so many soldiers and monsters to his army that we were simply overwhelmed by their numbers."

"Prince Calford!" shouts a knight, approaching hurriedly. "A courier slipped through the enemy's ranks! He brought news from Balshad!"

The courier, obviously injured, kneels beside Calford. With a shock, you recognize Ildrith, Rynath's younger brother. Ildrith glances uncertainly at Ayrsayle, then reports, "My lord, Rampillion's lava warriors are at the very gates of the royal castle! Balshad must receive aid soon, or it will surely fall!"

His urgent message delivered, Ildrith sinks to the ground, unconscious. Only then do you

see the arrow stuck in his side. Rynath rushes
to her brother's side to treat his wound.

"Should we go to Balshad's aid immediately,
or should we attack the Zorians now, then fly
to Balshad?" you ask excitedly.

"Perhaps you can do both at once," Calford
replies thoughtfully. "If you could compose a
spell to use against the Zorians, you could
send your scaly friend here to Balshad immediately to stop the lava warriors."

"Perhaps I could," you murmur. "I still have
the manual of sorcery. . . ."

1) If you decide to attack the Zorians, turn
to page 60.

2) If you decide to try to use the book of
spells against the Zorians, turn to page
148.

All around you, people are running through the streets in fear and confusion. As you search the sky for the circling dragon, you try to remain calm. If the book's spell brought Fyrewhyp to life, it must contain magic strong enough to defeat the red dragon.

"What did you do, Treon?" Rynath demands from behind you. You almost jump out of your skin, not realizing she was there.

"I—I conjured up a dragon," you explain, shame-faced. "I read a spell out loud without realizing what I was doing. Now I've got to find a spell to get rid of it before it roasts everything in sight."

The street darkens under a gigantic shadow, and you hear an earth-shattering roar. You dodge bolts of flame as you zigzag across the open courtyard, with Rynath at your heels.

You duck behind a cart filled with apples and frantically flip through the pages of the book. A bolt of fire shoots past the cart, singeing your hair.

Again you see the shadow of Fyrewhyp's huge wings along the ground as the gigantic dragon climbs upward to make another pass at you.

As you and the elf crouch in terror, Fyrewhyp swoops by again, setting fire to a nearby building.

Once more your mind reels as you grope for a solution. "Do you think I could try a spell to free Ayrsayle from my ring to battle Fyrewhyp?" you ask Rynath desperately. "Or

should I try to reverse the original spell that brought Fyrewhyp to life?"

"I don't know," she cries, "but whatever you do, you had better do it fast!"

1) If you decide to summon Ayrsayle from your ring to battle Fyrewhyp, turn to page 114.

2) If you try to reverse the spell that made Fyrewhyp appear, turn to page 55.

"I must retain my dragon form awhile longer!" you declare.

"Treon, no!" your mother gasps, startled at your answer.

"Mother, this whole situation is my fault!" you hasten to explain. "But by defeating Fyrewhyp—with help from you and Daphal—I have been able to correct some of my mistakes. Now the dragon book can provide a new weapon to use against Rampillion—me!"

"You have already risked your life in battle once today, my son," your mother says slowly. "Isn't that enough to ask of my youngest child?"

"Mother, what choice do we have?" you ask. "Rampillion's lava soldiers are poised to attack, most of the royal army is at the Zorian border, and part of the outer defenses of the castle have been destroyed!"

"But the dragon spell could become permanent, Treon," Daphal reminds you. "You might have to live the rest of your life as a dragon!"

"I would rather be a brave dragon than a would-be wizard who starts more trouble than he can stop!" you say firmly.

You can tell by looking at your mother that her determination is weakening. Her shoulders slump in resignation, but there is an expression of fierce pride in her eyes.

Please turn to page 70.

"I've got to go after Rampillion, Mother!" you roar as you spread your wings and rise into the air after dropping off your mother and Rynath. "If I can defeat the Crimson Wizard, I'll make up for all the trouble I've caused!"

"Treon, wait! Rampillion is a powerful wizard, with many years of experience. You are only a novice," your mother shouts. "As your mother and your queen, I order you to return!"

"Sorry, but dragons don't obey humans," you call back. "Wish me luck!" You flap in a powerful, regular rhythm as you search the mountains that ring the capital city. Finally you spot the Crimson Wizard on top of Mount Hood. He is waving his staff in the air and chanting.

When Rampillion sees you, he stops long enough to shout, "So this is the cowardly dragon who refused to fight Fyrewhyp in a fair battle!" He laughs evilly and continues to wave his staff.

"I'll show you how cowardly I am, Rampillion!" you roar. Angrily you turn in midair and dive at the wizard. When you are still a hundred feet away, you breathe a bolt of dragonfire straight at him.

To your amazement, the flames pass right through Rampillion's body! Then you see the form of the Crimson Wizard standing on the next summit. He has tricked you with an illusion of himself, a simple second-level spell!

Enraged at being fooled, you climb back into the air and land on the next mountain peak, claws extended. Your jaws open wide to snap the evil wizard in two. Instead, you find yourself biting into a small tree. You spit out the splinters and stringy bark in disgust.

"What's the matter, young dragon—or shall I call you by your real name, Treon?" the brightly robed sorcerer calls smugly from a third peak, his arms folded around his magical staff. "Do you want to do battle or not? I don't have time for childish games."

Billowing flames and roaring a booming challenge, you launch into the air again. But once more you find yourself attacking an illusion. Infuriated, you attack Rampillion's image again and again, until your wings ache and your dragonfire is only a tiny flame at the back of your throat.

"I'll land on this mountain to rest," you tell yourself. "I won't react to his insults until I'm sure Rampillion is really standing someplace."

Gratefully, you clutch solid ground. You sink your claws into the rocky soil and take a deep breath. You had not realized that even dragons can become tired. Every muscle seems to ache as you force your body to relax.

Suddenly you feel your wings begin to stiffen, and your legs grow sluggish and heavy. You try to turn your head, but you can't move. In desperation, you notice the golden scales of your body fading to a rocky gray!

"Poor apprentice wizard," Rampillion clucks, his voice heavy with sarcasm. "So easily insulted and so quickly worn out. But to work my petrifying spell properly, I needed my victim to be motionless and too weak to resist."

The Crimson Wizard walks right up to your stiffened form and taps your leg with his staff. It makes a dull, hard sound, as though he were hitting Mount Hood itself.

He studies the profile of your stone dragon body and then looks down at the now helpless city of Balshad.

"Yes, this will make a wonderful addition to the skyline as I look out from the royal castle," Rampillion says. "A new monument to the power of my sorcery—Mount Treon!"

THE END

"You're my only chance to escape," you say to the dragon ring. "I can't be in much more trouble than I am now!"

"You must combine your magical powers with mine to make the spell powerful enough," Ayrsayle tells you.

You finish tracing the words of the spell in the dust of the tower floor just as you hear the orcs unlock the prison cell. Signaling the tiny dragon, you chant in unison:

"Let Rampillion's magic now rescind;
  No longer trap this dragon ring.
  We break the curse; now float the wind,
  And take us under dragon's wing!"

You feel a tingling in your ring finger, then a steady pulsing that grows more powerful by the second. Finally the tiny dragon that is Ayrsayle raises his wings and flies right off your finger.

You take a wooden bench from the floor of your cell and barricade the door to try to keep out the guards. The guards push through the barricade and enter the cell. One orc slashes at you with a curved scimitar, while the other advances toward you with a menacing battle-ax.

You risk a quick glance back at Ayrsayle to see that the dragon is growing at a fantastic rate. Quickly you duck between her legs to avoid being crushed.

The amazed orcs retreat down the stairs as

Ayrsayle's growing body bursts open the top of your cell. Suddenly the floor gives way beneath your feet, and you fall helplessly toward the bottom floor far below. Gigantic blocks of stone hurtle down around you, and you scream in terror as you plunge earthward. Ayrsayle's great bulk has destroyed the tower—and taken you along with it!

All at once you feel powerful claws grab you in midair. Ayrsayle, her golden scales gleaming, holds you safely in her grip.

You watch the fragments of the tower crashing down to the castle floor below, sending startled orcs and humans stumbling in confusion.

"You have freed me from the curse of the ring. I am greatly in your debt," the huge dragon booms. "How may I help you in return, Treon?"

"You've gotten off to an awfully good start just now by saving me from certain death," you say. "But if you can, help me to return to Trigedium to find Rynath. She'll know how best to use your power."

"No sooner said than done, Treon. We can return to your friend in minutes through the magic portal near the Zorian border," Ayrsayle says.

She flies straight toward the stone pinnacle sticking up from the desert. When it seems as if you surely must crash into it, you simply disappear into thin air. After several moments of terrifying nothingness, you suddenly reappear high in the air directly over Trigedium.

You land on the outskirts of the city and hurry through the streets as the golden dragon crisscrosses in the air above you. Stopping at the Inn of the Rising Phoenix, you recruit a group of royal soldiers and lead them to Madam Ursula's bookery.

Bursting into the book shop with swords held ready, the warriors find only Rynath, tied up in the back room.

"What happened?" you ask the elf, checking your tutor for injuries as you quickly untie her.

"When I came back here to check on you, two orcs knocked me out," Rynath says, rubbing her head. "I was alone and tied up when I came to. Where did you go?"

"I wound up in Zor," you say.

"How did you get THERE?"

"By magic portal, I suspect," you answer. "At least that's how I got back here."

Rynath's face looks blank. Quickly you explain about Madam Ursula's true identity and your summoning of Ayrsayle. After you finish telling your story, you search the bookery for the manual of sorcery and discover it on the counter where you left it. Unless you miss your guess, it could prove to be very handy!

You stuff the manual of sorcery into your shoulder pouch and leave the bookery to rejoin Ayrsayle at the edge of town.

Rynath watches in awe as Ayrsayle lands in

front of you in a field by the road. You introduce the elf and the dragon to each other and explain to Ayrsayle what happened at the book shop.

"And there was no sign of the Crimson Wizard?" Ayrsayle sighs, disappointed. "Then once more he has escaped my revenge, after all these years!"

"You'll get your chance if I have anything to do about it!" you say determinedly. "You can help us track down the Crimson Wizard. As I see it, he's probably in one of two places. He might be with his army of lava warriors preparing to attack our capital, Balshad. Or he might have gone to the Zorian front to lead his army of orcs and human mercenaries against the royal army."

Flames roar from Ayrsayle's mouth, and her eyes gleam fiercely. "Climb up on my back, both of you! We have a score to settle with that evil wizard! Where shall I take you, Treon?"

1) If you think Rampillion joined his lava warriors at Balshad, turn to page 79.

2) If you think the Crimson Wizard went to the Zorian battlefront, turn to page 52.

"We must wait for Daphal to contact us," your mother sighs. "Mind links sent from a distance use a great deal of magical power. I hope Rampillion doesn't detect her sorcery."

"Now that we've defeated Fyrewhyp, are we just going to sit around?" you fume.

"Even dragons need rest, Treon," your mother says gently.

"Hmmmf!" you snort. But soon your exhausting fight with the red dragon catches up with you. Wearily you curl your body around the ruined battlements of the outer castle walls and fall into a deep sleep.

You don't know how long you've slept when you feel Rynath prodding you awake. Immediately Rynath straps two special dragon saddles to your neck.

"I finally heard from Daphal," your mother says. "She trailed Rampillion through a tunnel inside Mount Hood. He is now out of the tunnel and escaping through the forest on the other side. Daphal told me that much, but then her thought ended suddenly in midsentence. I fear the Crimson Wizard may have discovered her!"

Rynath climbs into one saddle, then stretches out a hand to Queen Niade, who holds her magical staff in one hand. "Quickly, Treon! Your sister may be in great danger!" your mother urges.

In the pale moonlight, you fly over the ring of mountains surrounding Balshad, then circle Mount Hood several times. Your mother moves her staff through the air slowly, chanting a detect magic spell. Suddenly she stiffens, as though listening to something.

"I have located Daphal," she says finally, sighing with relief. "She is unhurt, but I seem to detect she can't move. Rampillion must have discovered her and frozen her with a spell. I feel it must be merely a temporary spell, because the wizard was in a weakened condition himself. The sorcery will probably wear off in minutes."

Looking down, you spot Daphal's unmoving body. But then you notice something else— a scrap of telltale red cloth hanging from a bush about a hundred feet from your sister. Suddenly you spot movement in the pine trees.

"I've located Rampillion!" you announce. "It's time to smoke out the evil wizard!"

You dive to treetop level and shower the forest with dragonfire as your mother casts a shield spell around Daphal to protect her. You bank against the night breeze and breathe more flames over the wooded section where you saw the scrap of crimson robe.

All at once, Rampillion, coughing uncontrollably, stumbles out of the burning forest, beating out his smoking clothes and singed beard.

"Now it's time to cast a freezing spell!" The queen weaves her arms and chants the incantation, paralyzing the Crimson Wizard where he stands. A wisp of smoke trails up behind him as his sorcerer's hat crumbles into ashes.

Swiftly swooping down and plucking him

from the mountainside, you head for Balshad, with Daphal in one claw and a motionless Rampillion in the other. You land gently in the courtyard of the royal city, where royal guards lock the frozen wizard in the strongest dungeon in the castle. Your mother tends to Daphal, and soon your sister is free of the spell cast on her.

The people of the city rejoice Fyrewhyp's defeat and Rampillion's capture with a huge celebration. Stretched out on the ramparts of the outer wall of the castle, you receive choice food and lavish praise.

But some time later, after restudying transformation magic and trying several counterspells, your mother has bad news for you.

"I'm afraid we waited too long, Treon," she tells you sadly. "It looks as if you've become a dragon permanently."

"I'll be a dragon for the rest of my life?" you ask, shocked. For a moment, you want to crawl into a dark cave and never come out again. Then you remember the thrill of soaring through the clouds and the cheering of the people proclaiming you "Hero of Balshad."

"I suppose I'll have to get used to my new self," you say. "Perhaps being the only dragon in the country is better than being the fifth child of its rulers and its most unlucky apprentice wizard!"

THE END

High above, you see Fyrewhyp circling among the clouds. Then suddenly the huge dragon dips sharply and dives straight at you.

Quickly you hold up your ring to the sun and chant:

> "Let ancient magic of this tale
> No longer trap in dragon ring.
> I break the curse. Now fly, Ayrsayle,
> And take me under dragon's wing."

Just as you finish, Fyrewhyp unleashes a huge jet of flame straight toward you and Rynath. You close your eyes, expecting the worst.

But instead of searing heat against your face, you feel only cool air and the pleasant sensation of being gently cradled.

You open your eyes to see yourself surrounded by mist. You fear the worst, until suddenly the mist clears, and you realize you are emerging from a cloud bank. Looking up in astonishment, you see an enormous gold-scaled dragon holding you and Rynath securely in its claws.

"How did we get up here?" you shout in surprise.

"Unless I am mistaken, your former ring saved us," Rynath replies.

"FORMER ring?" you cry. You glance at your ring finger, now bare.

"You are safe with me, Treon," the huge dragon thunders. "But why did you summon forth Fyrewhyp? His type of dragon gives my race a bad name."

As the great golden dragon glides to a landing, you realize with a shock that she is the same dragon who was held captive in your ring. You can hardly believe your magic set her free.

"Did—did I really summon you to life?" you ask Ayrsayle timidly.

She drops you lightly on your feet and then soars skyward. "Yes, young wizard. You have freed me from Rampillion's curse. In return, I go now to battle Fyrewhyp." The dragon circles majestically above you. "I would welcome your help, young wizard. Fyrewhyp is a powerful foe. Stand by and be prepared to use what magic you can."

You hadn't really expected this. Could you, a mere apprentice magic-user, really be of help to the mighty Ayrsayle? So far, you seem to have done more harm than good. . . .

1) If you think you should leave the battle to the two dragons, turn to page 29.

2) If you decide to search in your manual of sorcery for a spell to help Ayrsayle against Fyrewhyp, turn to page 89.

"Pull up, Ayrsayle!" you yell as the mountain slope looms dangerously near.

"What about Rampillion?" Rynath shouts.

"I'm not powerful enough to face him," you reply, shaking your head, "even if he is in a weakened condition."

You realize you have let the worst enemy your country has ever had slip away. Now you must concentrate on stopping the erupting volcano and the lava warriors.

Ayrsayle banks sharply to avoid another shower of rock missiles from the lava monsters below.

"Ayrsayle, you said the magic portals work to change time as well as place. Open the magic portal to prehistoric times," you tell the dragon.

A curtain of rainbows covers the top of the volcano. The molten lava and fierce lava warriors disappear, leaving the volcano in a calm, quiet state.

"What happened?" Rynath gasps.

"We sent the lava warriors marching straight into the past! With any luck, the dinosaurs will take care of them!"

You fly back to Balshad to help the royal army against the remaining attackers. Without Rampillion's leadership, the lava warriors flee in terror before Ayrsayle's mighty strength.

You land, weary but victorious, outside the city gates to face the cheering crowd. Your mother steps forward, smiling broadly.

"Don't become too relaxed in your moment of triumph," Ayrsayle warns her. "Somewhere a powerful wizard nurses a grudge against you. Sooner or later, Rampillion will return seeking revenge!"

"We will be prepared," your mother says calmly, glancing your way.

Something about the way she says it puzzles you. "We?" you repeat, wondering at her meaning.

"Yes, my son," she goes on, smiling proudly. "Study the manual of sorcery well, and I have the feeling I shall not be Grendopolan's reigning wizard for long!"

THE END

"I've finally got enough power to correct the mistakes I've made," you tell Rynath. "Now I'm going to do something about it!" Thrilled at the strength of your powerful new body, you fly toward Balshad.

"But is strength enough, without wisdom to guide it?" Rynath cautions.

Ignoring Rynath's question, you scan the skies for the winged menace you are responsible for bringing here.

Nearing Balshad, evidence of Fyrewhyp's presence isn't difficult to spot. The walls of the castle are ablaze in several places. Apparently the queen's magic has repelled the beast from the city itself, but Fyrewhyp is now making a shambles of Balshad's outer defenses.

You fly straight at Fyrewhyp, roaring a challenge at the top of your lungs. Warned by your cry, the enormous dragon rolls in midair and manages to escape your first stream of fiery breath.

Again you dive at your enemy, but this time you barely avoid crashing into the burning castle walls. Your human brain still doesn't know how to control your gigantic wings, and once more Fyrewhyp escapes you.

Sensing your clumsiness, time and again the red dragon rakes you with its claws and fangs while dodging your awkward attempts to defend yourself.

Finally, in a furious attack, the red dragon's wing knocks Rynath from your back. Fighting back the pain of your wounds, you swoop down to catch your friend, but as you do, you expose your defenseless back to Fyrewhyp. It is all the opportunity the evil monster needs.

As you pluck the elf from the air, you feel Fyrewhyp's talons dig deep into your back. You have made your last mistake. And, unlike your other mistakes, you won't get any more chances this time. . . .

THE END

"I guess I'd better not risk using the spell book," you say reluctantly. "It might backfire and cause more trouble."

You and Rynath hurry into the small cave. Rynath takes position by the opening, to keep an eye on how the battle is progressing. "Calford's men seem to be holding their own," Rynath says, staring out the opening. Then she sucks in her breath and says, "Uh-oh! Guess who just arrived?"

"Who?" you whisper as you move to her side. Your ring finger begins to tingle.

"Well, well. The young prince does turn up in the most unexpected places," says a sinister voice. "Come out and meet the mighty Rampillion face-to-face!"

Panic-stricken, you hesitate as you try desperately to come up with some kind of plan. The evil wizard grows impatient, raises his magical staff, and chants a spell. Immediately rocks begin to crash down all around you as the top of the cave crumbles down on you. Coughing and sputtering, you and Rynath stumble out of the cave before you are buried alive.

A tall, bearded figure stands before you, laughing evilly. Then his face hardens to a mask of cruelty. "You have caused me much trouble, young prince." Rampillion's eyes dart to the spell book you clutch to your side. "How thoughtful! You have brought me my favorite book!"

The Crimson Wizard snaps his fingers, and

you feel the manual of sorcery leap from your fingers and fly into his hands. "This will be useful in disposing of your dragon friend! Ayrsayle was able to save you before, but this time none of you will escape!"

His eyes glow evilly as he weaves his hands, chants a string of magic, then points his fingers straight at you. You feel your body begin to shrink. You call desperately to Rynath for help, but your elven tutor is shrinking along with you. In a few terrifying moments, you find yourself nothing more than a decorative bauble on the finger of your archenemy.

THE END

"Calford's mounted troops should be able to manage by themselves for a while," you say. "We should be able to rescue Erik and return to help the royal army within a day. On to Lerthune, Ayrsayle!"

You fly across the blazing desert sky until you spot the low, sandstone fortress of Rampillion on the edge of the Zorian city. Ayrsayle lands in a small, rocky valley to avoid being spotted.

"Most dungeons have several different underground levels," Rynath says. "If we attack with Ayrsayle, the Crimson Wizard's guards may have time to kill the prisoners before we can rescue them."

"How do we get past the guarded city gates to get to Erik's cell, then?" you ask.

"I didn't give you lessons in avoiding detection all these years for nothing, Treon," the elf chides you. "Ayrsayle will have to stay behind and keep out of sight."

"I can keep in mind contact with you, young prince," Ayrsayle says. "As long as you can reach an open window or an outside door, I can make contact and come to your rescue if necessary."

You and Rynath start off across the burning sands, being careful to stay low behind the cover of the windswept dunes. As you near the city, the desert sands give way to irrigated fields. You come upon a loaded hay wagon and, guessing that the owner will soon be taking it into the city, decide to hide in it.

Your guess soon proves to be correct as you feel the wagon begin to roll slowly toward the city. Once inside the city, you leap out under cover of another passing wagon and make your way to the formidable building that surely must be the dungeon. Finding a guard asleep outside an entrance, you quietly slip by him into the building.

You and Rynath cautiously make your way through the dim passages of the dungeon. As you pass through an open chamber, you hear rats scurrying by and bats flapping their wings overhead.

"I wonder why we haven't seen any more guards," you whisper. "Even if most of the soldiers have gone off with the invading army, the dungeon shouldn't be this empty."

"I think I just found out why," says Rynath as she peers around the corner of a dark stairwell.

You look, too, and what you see makes your blood run cold. "What is THAT?" you ask in horror. A seven-foot-long spider scurries back and forth in front of the prisoner's cells.

"It's a tarantella!" Rynath exclaims. "Its bite doesn't kill, but it causes a painful spasm that resembles a frantic dance."

Just then you hear someone shout, "Intruders have breached the dungeon walls! Find them and kill them on sight!"

"Should we get to a window and call for Ayrsayle?" you ask nervously. "There are a lot of walls between us and the door we entered."

"If we subdue the tarantella now, we might be able to free Erik," Rynath says. "If we try to come back later, the guards are sure to be waiting for us."

1) If you call Ayrsayle and try to escape the dungeon immediately, turn to page 62.

2) If you decide to battle the tarantella and try to free Erik, turn to page 13.

"I don't think I have enough experience to face a master wizard like Rampillion, even with Ayrsayle on our side," you admit to Rynath. "I'm still only an apprentice."

"That's the first good sense you've shown," the elf agrees. "But how will you stop this supernatural eruption?"

You glance around you. The air is so thick with cinders and swirling ashes that your eyes water. Blinking rapidly, you flip through the pages of the dragon manual, trying to read through your tears.

"I may have found something," you say excitedly. "The spell is actually designed to stop dragonfire, though, so I'll have to adjust the wording."

"You'd better hurry," Rynath cautions. "I think Rampillion is up to something."

Not knowing what might happen if the spell doesn't work, you chant:

"Let ancient fires flow no more
And magic seal the fiery door!"

Suddenly you feel the air begin to cool. The cone of the volcano below slowly turns from fiery red, to pink, then to the normal color of rock. The lava warriors, their magical energy source gone, slowly freeze in place, like stone monuments.

"Begone, Rampillion!" Ayrsayle thunders. "Your army exists no more. Leave, while you still can."

"I will leave, dragon!" Rampillion snarls, "but I will return!" And with a puff of brilliant red smoke, the Crimson Wizard disappears.

"I'm afraid you will have to face him in the future, Treon," Ayrsayle says.

"But by then, I should be an experienced royal wizard," you reply. "For the time being, at least, the kingdom is safe."

THE END

"You are the ranking wizard and have by far the most experience," you say to your mother. "If you think we should wait here and join forces against Rampillion's army, we will."

The hours drag on as the citizens of Balshad try to repair the outer wall of the castle that was destroyed in Fyrewhyp's flaming attack.

Just as the sun sets, hordes of lava warriors pour from the forest and advance toward the city.

"Come on, Treon," Daphal shouts as she and Rynath climb onto your neck. "It's time to earn our keep!"

You rise into the sky above Balshad, then swoop down on the lumbering lava creatures and attack them with your dragonfire. Daphal casts freeze spells, cooling the weird creatures to stone statues, whenever she can summon enough energy.

It soon grows obvious, however, that too many invaders are slipping by. They charge through the ruined sections of the outer wall and begin to overpower the royal troops. Their thick lava hides glisten in the fading sunlight as the creatures swing their stone clubs.

Diving through the growing darkness, you suddenly crash into unseen strands that immediately wrap themselves around you. You struggle to remain in the air, but your efforts seem to entangle you in the ropelike strands even more.

"Rampillion must have hurled an advanced-level web spell!" Daphal cries.

Before long, your wings are hopelessly tangled in the web, and you plummet helplessly toward the earth.

You slam into the dirt, and pain shoots through one of your wings. Immediately dozens of heavy rock creatures weigh you down and take Daphal and Rynath prisoner.

"So this is the golden dragon who is foolish enough to try to save Balshad!" a sinister voice cackles. Clad in crimson robes and holding a staff, Rampillion advances toward you.

You struggle to break free, but the rock warriors hold you down. Wrapped tightly around your jaws, the magical webbing prevents you from using your dragonfire.

"You don't act like a true dragon somehow," Rampillion says suspiciously. "Perhaps you are not who you seem to be."

Rampillion scans your mind, the way Daphal did after you freed her. "Why, it's the youngest prince of Grendopolan, playing with spells beyond his comprehension!" the Crimson Wizard gloats triumphantly as he discovers your true identity.

"Fortunately I have dealt with transformation spells before!" Rampillion chortles. The evil wizard chants a spell in the ancient dragon language and waves his magical staff. You feel your front left paw begin to tringle, and once more you experience the strange supernatural storm.

As the unnatural wind subsides, you look down at your now human body. Laughing at

your helplessness, the lava warriors tie you up and push you roughly over to Daphal and Rynath, who are bound like you.

You watch helplessly as Rampillion's army overruns Balshad. Then the Crimson Wizard locks you and your family in the dungeon, after casting a dispel magic spell on your mother and your sisters, robbing them of their magical powers.

"I think you've learned your lesson about casting spells beyond your ability, haven't you, young prince?" Rampillion gloats as the door clanks shut.

As the evil wizard moves off down the corridor, you hear him speak of his battle plans against your brothers and the royal army at the Zorian border.

Suddenly you realize that the lava warriors failed to search you. You glance over your shoulder and note with growing hope that your shoulder pouch is back again, now that you've regained your human form. Quickly you glance down at your hand. Madame Ursula's dragon ring is back on your finger!

You check to make sure no guards are watching, then pull the book of spells from your pouch and begin to flip through the pages.

"Yes, I've learned my lesson, Crimson Wizard," you say slowly. "And I'm going to know exactly what I am doing when I cast my next spell!"

THE END

You decide that no matter how much stronger the ring might make you, with your limited knowledge of magic, it wouldn't help as much as even a few new spells. You can hardly wait to examine it as you blurt out, "I'll buy the book!"

As Madam Ursula steadies your hand to try to remove the ring, one of the dragon's fangs pricks your finger.

"I'm sorry! I should have been more careful!" Madam Ursula says, leaving the ring on your finger. "Now I see that one tooth does stick out a bit."

A drop of blood appears in the wound, although it doesn't hurt.

"We don't want that to fester," Madam Ursula says as she examines the wound. "Come into the back room, and I'll wash and bandage it for you."

You glance questioningly at Rynath, who nods her approval. As you follow the old woman, you notice several clerics in long gray robes with hoods over their heads enter the bookery.

In the back room, you see even more fascinating items than in the shop. Drawings and sculptures of dragons are everywhere. On one table, you see beakers and vials that look like the equipment your sister Daphal uses when she creates magic potions. You inspect everything curiously.

You look down at the dragon ring still on your finger and notice an inscription under the dragon's wing. "A-Y-R-S-A-Y-L-E," you spell out silently.

You sit down in a wooden rocking chair and ask, "What does 'Ayrsayle' mean?"

"Ayrsayle! Where did you hear that name?" Madam Ursula asks nervously, a look of fear in her eyes.

You hold up your left hand. "The name is on the ring," you say, puzzled at her reaction.

"Oh, that!" Madam Ursula says, sounding relieved. She appears to think for a moment before replying. "That's how my name is spelled back in my home country."

"Where are you from?" you ask. Now that you think of it, her accent doesn't sound like she grew up in Grendopolan.

"Originally I came from Sherinad," the old woman answers.

"But—but that's the island where all the dragons came from!" you exclaim. "And Sherinad was destroyed hundreds of years ago. You couldn't be that old!"

"Young lord, you must never question a lady about her age," the woman scolds, "even if I am only a humble bookery owner."

Something about the way Madam Ursula acts reminds you of a dragon more than a book shop owner. She moves with a quiet, powerful grace that seems to hypnotize you, the way dragons can do.

You shake your head and decide to change the subject. " 'Ayrsayle' doesn't sound like it's from any human language," you say. "It reminds me of the few words I know from the old dragon language. Do you understand the dragon tongue?"

"My, my, but you are curious, young man," Madam Ursula says. The old woman shakes her head and clucks her tongue. She washes your finger in an earthen bowl that smells like tangerines.

"What's that?" you ask as she takes a bottle from a table of beakers bubbling over candle flames and carefully unstoppers it.

"Just a medicinal brew to help heal your wound," Madam Ursula answers. "It may sting a little."

You begin to feel oddly uneasy about the old woman. What if the 'medicinal brew' is part of some magical spell that Madam Ursula is about to cast? What if it's poison? Maybe you should get up and get out of here as quickly as possible.

1) If you decide to leave the back room of the shop at once and rejoin Rynath, turn to page 72.

2) If, instead, you put aside your fears and trust Madam Ursula to put the healing liquid on your finger, turn to page 83.

You remember Rynath's advice in the bookery about using knowledge wisely. It was your ignorance that caused Fyrewhyp to appear. Daphal is the closest source of magical wisdom to help correct your mistake.

You arch your wings away from the fiery battle raging over Balshad and turn toward the slopes of Mount Enam, where you last saw your sister. A short burst of crackling yellow energy lights up the mountain slope in the distance.

"Daphal must have managed to conjure up a spell in spite of everything," you say excitedly. You realize how powerful your sister truly is, even in her weakened state.

Swooping low, you see your sister, surrounded by lava warriors. One lies stunned, while another guard circles her menacingly. A third lava warrior swings his stone war club at Daphal's head. She ducks under the fierce blow, but as she does, a fourth soldier trips her with his spear.

"Kill her!" yells yet another of the glowing lava creatures. "She's caused too much trouble, and Rampillion wouldn't get any information out of her anyway."

"She's used too much of her magical strength to free herself, Treon," Rynath shouts. "Your sister is helpless now!"

You dive through the air toward the fearsome creatures below. As if by instinct, you purse your lips, and fiery breath streams out in front of you. Four lava warriors disappear

in a wall of flame, and the other two lumbering creatures stumble off awkwardly in panic.

Daphal turns toward you, obviously weak, and waves her trembling hands, preparing to hurl a spell at you.

"Save your magic for our enemies, Daphal!" you shout as you glide to a landing. "It looks like I'm finally going to get to help you out for once," you add to your startled sister.

"Ah . . . Treon, I don't think she recognizes you," Rynath points out, then turns to Daphal. "Greetings, Princess Daphal," she calls.

Daphal seems to notice the figure astride your back for the first time. "Rynath?" she asks, puzzled. "How came you by this dragon?"

"Your brother Treon conjured him forth," your tutor answers. "It was the only way he could get help against Fyrewhyp."

"Fyrewhyp?" Daphal repeats blankly.

"Fyrewhyp is . . . uh . . . the other dragon," Rynath tries to explain, realizing she isn't making much sense.

"There's ANOTHER dragon loose?" your sister gasps. "Just what have you been doing? And where is Treon, anyway?"

"I—I am Treon," you gulp. Daphal retreats a few steps, then stares blankly at you.

"We don't have any time to explain," you go on. "Use your mind scan, Daphal. You'll know I am telling the truth."

Daphal stares into your eyes intently and rubs her temples. Finally she appears to be satisfied and approaches to within a few feet of your lowered snout.

"How were you captured, Daphal?" you ask.

"I was leading a scouting party to find out where the lava warriors are coming from." Daphal rubs the angry-looking burns that the rope left on her arms. Rynath bandages your sister's wounds while Daphal continues.

"A patrol of lava warriors ambushed my group as we were returning from Enam. We didn't discover how Rampillion is creating those monsters, but we did discover something almost as important.

"The attack from Zor is merely a diversion, meant to divide the royal army's strength," Daphal explains. "The main force of the attack will come from the army of lava warriors Rampillion has created magically within the bowels of Enam."

You claw the earth angrily with your talons. "Let's go," you cry suddenly.

"Go where, Treon?" Daphal asks, halting you with an upraised hand. "I sense that too much haste was the cause of all these dragons appearing in the first place."

"But—but Fyrewhyp is attacking Balshad at this very minute!" Rynath cries.

"And Rampillion is leading his lava warriors in a full-scale assault on the city through a hidden crevice between Enam and neighboring Mount Hood, just outside the very gates of the city itself," Daphal replies. "We must stop them before they reach Balshad!"

As one, Rynath and your sister turn to face you. "Treon, the tide of battle must lie with you," Daphal says slowly. "Your newly acquired strength and your apparent command of this ancient sorcery are our only hopes. But where shall we attack?"

1) If you decide to attack Fyrewhyp first, so that a united Balshad can face Rampillion's invading lava army, turn to page 41.

2) If you decide to ambush the lava warriors before they reach the city, turn to page 91.

"Although it seems crazy to leave Ayrsayle, this may be our only chance to capture Rampillion," you decide. "He must be tired from overusing his magical powers. I doubt if he can stay invisible for long."

With a gigantic flash of dragonfire, Ayrsayle sends the lava warriors lumbering for cover, clearing a safe landing space. She lets you off on the volcano's slope near the place where you last saw Rampillion, then circles above you to keep watch.

Rynath uses her infravision to spot faint footprints, which lead up the slope toward the rim of the crater. You follow the trail, keeping watch for any returning lava warriors. As you near the lip of the volcano, Rampillion flashes into view above you. His invisibility spell must have worn off!

Suddenly a group of lava warriors appears below you, cutting off any possible escape. Your heart sinks to the pit of your stomach, but you form a desperate plan.

"Rynath," you whisper to the elf. "Stall him as long as you can. I've got an idea!"

"You forget, evil wizard, that Treon still has the manual of sorcery. Destroy us and you also destroy the book!" Rynath calls out.

The Crimson Wizard's eyes gleam at the thought of regaining this powerful weapon. Meanwhile, you begin to whisper the words of a transport spell.

"Young prince, I will spare your life in exchange for that book," Rampillion offers.

"Ayrsayle can't help you now. Her dragonfire would destroy you as well as us, standing this near to each other. A trade is your only hope of survival!"

You start to walk toward Rampillion, the book in your hands. As you near the rim of the crater, you suddenly dart toward it, as though to hurl the sorcery manual into its fiery pit. The magic portal mustn't fail you now!

The Crimson Wizard lunges to stop you and catches you on the edge of the crater. You grab him and struggle, teetering on the very edge. With your last ounce of strength, you pull him over the rim. As both of you fall toward what appears to be certain death, you chant the last line of the transport spell that will allow you to travel through the magic portal a few precious seconds into the past.

You blink back through the central portal just in time for Ayrsayle to swoop down and catch you. In her other front claw is Rynath.

Lacking your royal wizard's blood, Rampillion simply continues to fall into the fiery depths below. With his death, his power over the magic he has created dies, too. The molten lava and the weird lava creatures it spawned turn once more to stone.

Back in Balshad, cheering throngs of people wave to you as you approach. Your mother greets you outside the castle walls and thanks Ayrsayle for her help.

"But what has become of the manual of sorcery?" your mother asks.

"It fell into Enam in the struggle. I'm afraid it's gone forever."

"Perhaps that is for the best, Treon. If it were ever again to fall into the hands of some-one like the Crimson Wizard, it could cause irreparable harm. And now," she goes on, taking your hand, "it is time for a fitting celebration for a certain apprentice wizard who saved Balshad!"

THE END

"Help me to change back into a human," you urge your mother. "I—I've been a dragon long enough."

"Where is the manual of sorcery?" the queen asks. "We haven't a moment to lose." Daphal and Rynath, standing nearby, look at you expectantly.

"It's . . . uh . . . " You stop to think. You remember dodging bolts of fire outside the Rising Phoenix in Trigedium as you tried to reverse Fyrewhyp's spell. After that, you transported yourself to Balshad.

"I stuffed the book into my shoulder pouch for safekeeping!" you roar, frightening several villagers who have crept up to see you closer. Smoke belches from your nose in your excitement. "It's right here. . . ."

You arch your long, graceful neck toward your back. Suddenly you realize you have no shoulder, much less a shoulder pouch. You turn to your mother, panic-stricken.

"Treon, do you remember the exact spell that summoned Fyrewhyp and the counterspells you used afterward?" the queen asks.

"I—I think so, but I'm not positive," you gulp. "So much has happened today. . . ."

"You've got to try to be exact," your mother says firmly. "If you don't, you'll live out the rest of your life in the form of a dragon."

You repeat the spells word by word and phrase by phrase. You have to be careful not to say them in the exact order of the complete spell, remembering your unfortunate experience earlier. As you recall the words, your mother writes them down in a tablet, then spends a few minutes studying them. Finally she raises her head and has you repeat the incantation:

" 'Despite the errors of my tongue,
I now have beaten Fyrewhyp.
Remove the flames within my lungs.
My body send on homeward trip.' "

You grow dizzy as you whirl through icy blackness. Needles of electricity run up and down your ring finger. Finally the blackness clears to light, and you find yourself flat on your human back, staring up at your mother, sister, and Rynath.

"Welcome back, my son," your mother says with a smile. Then she leans down and kisses you on the cheek. "Are you all right?"

"I—I think so, except for this pain in my back," you groan.

"You're lying on top of your shoulder pouch," Daphal points out.

"My sorcerer's book!" you cry joyfully, jumping to your feet.

Your mother's eyes grow stern, and you remember all the trouble you have caused.

"This has all been my fault, Mother," you say slowly. "If I hadn't tampered with Madam Ursula's manual of sorcery, Fyrewhyp would have stayed just a page in a book. I'm ashamed to call myself an apprentice wizard."

"We all make mistakes when we try to learn any new skill. If you understand this and always try to correct them, as you did in that terrible battle in the sky, you may yet learn to be a great wizard," the queen says softly.

"Even with help from you and Daphal, Fyrewhyp still almost won," you groan. "I guess Rynath is right. I must use my brain to fight, not merely weapons."

"Rynath is a wise teacher," Niade replies as your tutor blushes.

"Now we must repair the castle walls to be ready for Rampillion and his lava warriors," Daphal reminds everyone. "At least we will be rested enough for our magical powers to be at full strength. Still, we could use any help we can get." She looks pointedly at the manual you hold in your hands.

"Now that you and Mother are here to teach me, perhaps I can learn to use this book correctly," you say. "And when the Crimson Wizard does arrive, we can have some nasty surprises ready for him!"

THE END

"Ayrsayle is our best weapon," you say to Calford. "But I think I can help you with my sorcery book while she flies to Balshad."

You watch the golden dragon until she is just a speck on the horizon.

"Thanks to the dragon, you've avoided getting into more trouble with your magic so far," Rynath reminds you. "Should you risk uncertain sorcery again? If it backfires, all is lost."

"But if Calford doesn't get some help right away, his outnumbered soldiers will be defeated anyway," you reply.

"The orcs are attacking!" a lookout shouts.

"To arms!" Calford cries. "Mount your steeds, brave knights! Rynath, you and Treon take cover in that cave in the cliff."

1) If you are reluctant to come to Calford's aid with a spell for fear of causing more trouble, turn to page 121.

2) If you are willing to risk using the manual of sorcery to formulate a spell, choose page 35.

"Fyrewhyp will reach Balshad long before we can hope to get there," you reason. "But if we free Daphal, her magic plus the power of my dragon ring might turn the tide of battle in our favor."

The weird lava warriors disappear around a bend in the mountain path as your mind races. "We've got to think of something soon," you say anxiously.

"Well, we certainly can't just march right straight up to them," Rynath says, looking worried. "One elf and one unarmed human would be no match for six of those strange creatures."

"Let's follow them. Maybe we'll be able to think of something along the way," you suggest.

The elf's skill at remaining undetected is valuable in trailing Daphal's captors. The lumbering rock creatures drag the struggling Daphal ever closer to the crater of Mount Enam. All the while, Fyrewhyp's dragonfire flashes brightly in the sky over Balshad.

"Rynath is right. We certainly can't overpower the monsters. We've got to outsmart them," you think.

"If ancient sorcery got us into this mess, it can get us out of it, too," you announce decisively, looking down at the dragon ring.

"Are you sure, my prince?" Your tutor looks doubtful. "The last time you attempted such magic, you released Fyrewhyp. Who knows what might happen this time?"

"Would you prefer to try to hold off all six lava warriors yourself while I help Daphal escape?"

Rynath heaves a sigh and shakes her head. The discussion has ended, and it is clear what you must do.

Please turn to page 31.

"Let's fly to the secret crevice," you decide. "Balshad has already received enough damage at the hands of Fyrewhyp. If we head off the lava warriors before they can attack, we can save the city from further destruction."

"But will even Treon's great strength be enough to stop a whole army of lava warriors?" Rynath asks, buckling on her battle armor.

"We'll use brains instead of brawn, the same way we defeated Fyrewhyp," Daphal replies.

"Treon, you know more about the dragons of Grendopolan than any of us do. What is the most terrible dragon in all history, a monster even the Crimson Wizard might fear?" Daphal asks.

You think for a moment, then reply, "That would have to be Lightningfang. Legends say that instead of breathing normal dragonfire, he shot fearsome bolts of crackling raw energy. Fortunately he was a lawful dragon, or nobody would be around to remember him."

"Then you will pretend to be Lightningfang," Daphal tells you.

"There are only two problems with that, Daphal," you protest. "He was silver, while I'm gold. And then there's the little matter that I don't shoot lightning bolts."

"I'll take care of your appearance," Daphal answers. "And I'll speak to our sister, Lira, about handling the lightning bolts."

"Where is Lira?" you ask, alarmed. "I haven't seen her. Is—is she all right?"

"Yes, Treon," your mother reassures you. "She became exhausted helping me hold off Fyrewhyp. I sent her to rest."

Lira is summoned, and soon your two sisters are deep in discussion. Unlike Daphal, Lira wears the brown robes of a cleric. Several soldiers arrive and begin to strap saddles onto your neck. You watch Lira anxiously as she nods at Daphal's plan and leaves.

Then Daphal and Rynath climb onto your neck. "Fly to Mount Enam, Treon," your sorcerer sister instructs you.

"Do you think Rampillion will still attack Balshad?" Rynath asks. "Maybe he saw what happened to Fyrewhyp, and it scared him off."

Daphal laughs in disbelief. "Not with the northern walls of the castle open to invasion!"

The cool air rushing by your face refreshes you, but you don't find your sister's words very comforting. Then suddenly the air turns darker, and you feel tiny cinders pricking your skin as you hover over Enam. "Look! I was right!" Daphal shouts, pointing.

Dozens of rocklike lava warriors are emerging from the hidden crevice. More of the strange creatures gather into ranks and receive orders from a tall human dressed in bright red robes.

"That's Rampillion, Daphal! Hang on tight! Here we go!" you shout, banking on the thermal winds to dive.

You feel heavy boots grind into your neck, and an oak staff smacks your ear. Yelping in pain, you level off, still hidden from below by the sooty clouds.

"Patience, Treon!" your sister snaps. "We have webs of trickery to weave before we face the Crimson Wizard."

"You'd better weave them fast, Daphal," you reply testily, your ears ringing from the blow of the heavy magical staff. "Those lava creatures are already marching toward Balshad, and more are pouring out of the volcano every minute!"

"They're marching through the valley between the mountains," Rynath reports as she peers through the clouds.

"Good!" Daphal says, to your surprise. "If that's the route they're taking, then my plan should work. Fly to the limestone quarry south of Balshad, Treon. Hurry!"

You arrive at the quarry, and immediately Daphal begins showing Rynath how to smear your hide with a sticky pine sap she has brought along. Then Daphal instructs you to roll around in the bottom of the limestone quarry until your golden scales have turned silvery white.

"Now you LOOK like Lightningfang, at least," Daphal says finally, nodding her approval.

As you fly back to the volcano, you wonder whether the ruse will work. When the volcano looms into sight, you see Rampillion's lava soldiers, now hundreds strong, marching toward Balshad.

"Now, Daphal?" you ask.

"No," your sister replies calmly. "Wait until they cross that large hill where the dwarves began digging a mine. Then we'll put our plan into action!"

In a grove of trees near the mine, you see Lira and her clerics performing some kind of ceremony. Overhead, you hear thunder rumble through the sky, which was clear only moments earlier.

"Excellent, Lira!" Daphal says, smiling, and you begin to understand her plan.

Just as the army of lava creatures covers the iron-filled slope, a lightning bolt flashes across the sky, striking within their midst with terrifying force. Two more jagged streaks of lightning soon follow. The lava warriors jump and howl in terror and confusion.

"Lira has set the stage for our dramatic entrance. Now, Treon!" Daphal yells.

In the gathering twilight, you swoop from the clouds in the twilight and dive straight for the Crimson Wizard. The force of air from your flapping wings knocks him to the ground as you hurtle past.

"Rampillion!" your sorcerer sister shouts. "I have conjured up the dreaded Lightningfang! If you and these monsters of your creation do not leave our world forever, I will have Lightningfang destroy you!"

Rampillion raises his staff and begins to chant a spell. Before he can finish, you see Lira below, working a minor illusion spell.

Her spell makes you appear to be shooting lightning, not flames, from your mouth.

The wizard looks shaken and pauses in mid-spell, his power wavering. At this instant, Lira and her clerics receive an answer to their prayers. A bolt of real lightning streaks down from the now turbulent skies, charring the magical staff in Rampillion's hands.

The lava warriors freeze in their tracks. You see that the hillside is now littered with rock statues of the strange monsters.

"I swear never to set foot in this wretched land again!" Rampillion shrieks, clutching his burned hands. And in a flash of red smoke, the Crimson Wizard disappears.

"Just in time, too!" You breathe a smoky sigh of relief. A driving rain begins to fall, washing away the limestone dust that covers your body.

"Will the Crimson Wizard keep his vow?" Rynath grumbles. "I don't trust him for one minute!"

"He has no choice," Daphal says. "A wizard who breaks his oath is stricken powerless forever. We are safe, thanks to Treon!"

"But it looks like I'll be a dragon from now on," you say sadly, spreading your wings and soaring through the clouds toward home.

"I don't think the people of Balshad will mind one bit," Daphal says, patting your back. "They will honor you as a hero, Treon!"

THE END

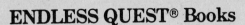

ENDLESS QUEST® Books

From the producers of the DUNGEONS & DRAGONS® Game

- **#1 DUNGEON OF DREAD**
- **#2 MOUNTAIN OF MIRRORS**
- **#3 PILLARS OF PENTEGARN**
- **#4 RETURN TO BROOKMERE**
- **#5 REVOLT OF THE DWARVES**
- **#6 REVENGE OF THE RAINBOW DRAGONS**
- **#7 HERO OF WASHINGTON SQUARE**
  based on the TOP SECRET® Game
- **#8 VILLAINS OF VOLTURNUS**
  based on the STAR FRONTIERS™ Game
- **#9 ROBBERS AND ROBOTS**
  based on the TOP SECRET® Game
- **#10 CIRCUS OF FEAR**
- **#11 SPELL OF THE WINTER WIZARD**
- **#12 LIGHT ON QUESTS MOUNTAIN**
  based on the GAMMA WORLD® Game
- **#13 DRAGON OF DOOM**
- **#14 RAID ON NIGHTMARE CASTLE**

For a free catalog, write:
TSR, Inc.
P.O. Box 756, Dept. EQB
Lake Geneva, WI 53147

TSR, Inc.